PRAISE FOR SKYWARD INN

"A powerful and surprising examination of colonialism and its unintended consequences. Highly recommended."
Helen Marshall, author of *The Migration*

"Intense and consuming writing, constantly challenging expectations."
Adrian Tchaikovsky, Arthur C. Clarke Award-winning author of *Children of Time*

"A story of the future that is an appeal to the present. The best kind of science fiction. A novel of its time, confronting current and terrible misjudgements with which humanity assures its own demise. All made startling by a typical Whiteley strangeness."
Adam Nevill, author of *The Reddening*

"Whiteley is one of the most original and provocative voices in contemporary science fiction."
Nina Allen, author of *The Rift*

"Visceral and unsettling—I loved it"
G. V. Anderson

PRAISE FOR ALIYA WHITELEY

"Whiteley has a penchant for describing the disturbing... a surreal and disquieting post-apocalyptic consideration of the roles we place ourselves in."
The Barnes and Noble SF&F Blog

"A murky delirium of sinuous language and unnerving storytelling that will delight both experienced genre fanatics and literary fiction lovers alike."
Kirkus Reviews

"Its triumph lies in the way Whiteley uses the metaphor to examine the tortured process of love and attachment."
The Guardian

"Aliya Whiteley is a philosopher, providing insights into the human psyche, opening up minds as she blows us away with beautiful prose."
The British Fantasy Society

First published 2021 by Solaris
an imprint of Rebellion Publishing Ltd,
Riverside House, Osney Mead,
Oxford, OX2 0ES, UK

www.solarisbooks.com

ISBN: 978 1 78108 882 1

A CIP catalogue record for this book is available from the
British Library.

Designed & typeset by Rebellion Publishing

Printed in the United Kingdom

ALIYA WHITELEY

SKYWARD INN

SOLARIS

For Anna and Shajeev

PART ONE

THEY'VE DRUNK THEIR drinks and sung their songs, and it's time for them to head for home. I wave them off, turn my back on the first streaks of light in the sky, and close the door to the inn.

Isley says, his voice soft and self-mocking, 'Alone at last.' He says it every time we've got the place to ourselves. He practised his English on Tung Base, millions of miles away, by watching old films, and sometimes I can imagine the kind of drama he thinks we're in. The lamps on the walls are burning low. I love this time, time between times. It's a soft grey bleed from night into morning.

'Pour,' I say. I walk back to the bar and pull up the well-used stool with the cracked leather top. The smell of the heaped glass ashtray between us is very strong, and I slide it to one side. The ash settles into the grooves patterning its rim.

The glasses Isley pulls out are his good ones. We're getting a taste from the best bottle. I smile when I see him lift it from under the counter—an automatic reaction to that conical shape, in the orange clay from his world.

'Special occasion?'

'You don't remember?' He pulls out the cork with his thick, blunt teeth and tips the clear liquid into the glasses. 'I thought you remembered everything.'

It's the thirteenth of September. It's not any anniversary I can think of, and we have drunk to them all.

'It's seven years since I first told you I love you,' he says, and clinks his glass against mine.

That was in this bar, and I was sitting on this very seat. His chin trembled when he said it, and I remember I thought only that I wanted him to not be scared of what comes next, of where love leads.

'I told you I loved you too,' I say. 'I didn't even have to think about it. The words came easily.'

'Are they still true?' He frowns into the glass he holds just below his mouth. When he drinks, the moment will be over with, done. It's impossible to feel bad with Jarrowbrew in your body.

'Everything I say to you is true,' I tell him, but it sounds unreal, so I add, 'At least, I try to make it that way.'

'You do try,' he agrees, 'and that's why I still love you now.'

It's a good thing to drink to. We drink.

Here it comes, here it is: the sweetness I associate with fields, and the depth I think of as the sea. The soft light it brings to my mind belongs to the sky of Qita. What do the regulars at our inn see, feel, when they drink brew, I wonder? Most of them have never been off this planet, or even out of the Westward Protectorate. They must translate it into their own experiences, which are no less potent, I'm thinking. Just—miniaturised. Pin-sharp, unshakeable, mired in the thick grasses of the West Country moor.

'Jem,' he says, 'You know Toulu? Where the rock divides? Did you ever go there?'

'I did.'

'Did you look at the fossils? In the heart of the rock?'

I fix Isley with my patient eyes. 'You know I did. I went to all the places, with my leaflets.'

'Yes,' he says softly. 'Your leaflets. Your letters of peace, from Earth to Qita. You put them up everywhere you went, for us to find.'

He sounds so sad. I give him what he wants, and what he never asks for, directly: a description of his homeworld. It's changed, of course. But here, right now, in my words, it hasn't. Not for us, on our different sides, meeting in the middle.

I say:

I remember Toulu.

Your creatures from your past, your fossils, are only shapes in old stone, so very far away. I put my hand on their outlines. I can tell you evolved from swimming organisms with long limbs and large domed heads; these were weighty bodies, leaving ribbed regular marks upon the rock, suggesting a shell. Your people have lost the shell through the path of time, just as humans did. Some things, we all have in common.

Toulu—the rock itself, a vast standing stone in a lake—was split by a great force, perhaps a natural event like lightning, leaving a clean edge. That, too, happened a long time ago. So there has been at least one act of violence on your gentle planet. A cataclysm of its time, for those creatures that lived near it; around it.

I was one of the first visitors to that place, and I was keen to suck up experiences of Qita, to better do my job of bridging the gap between us. When I saw it, I thought of how similar and how different it was from the earliest paintings made in caves here on Earth: Chauvet, Lascaux, Altamira, long cordoned off from casual visitors. They are far too precious to be worn down under the weight of endlessly curious humanity. Toulu is free, and open. I could never explain to anyone on this planet what it is like to have that genuine, amazing sight all to myself.

I spent time absorbed only in the marks of those long-dead bodies, frozen in the act of their own movement. They swam in perfect fractal patterns, proving—what? That Qita was always a planet of order, even down to its basic organisms?

I don't understand, even now. I never have.

I did not want to hang my message upon it, but that was my job, so I went ahead anyway. I used the nail gun to attach the leaflet. Not to the rock itself. To a nearby tree. But as I punctured its bark I thought: is this tree less beautiful? How long has it been standing here, keeping the rock company? They're an old married pair, and if I wound one, that injury will be mirrored in the other.

I put these thoughts down to my own ridiculousness, finished my job, and returned to the base. I made my report, and the regular tourist rides out to Toulu started soon after. *Military tourism keeps trouble at bay*, I was told.

'Jem?' says Isley, into the silence that follows. Jarrowbrew telescopes time as well as distance. It is, no doubt, morning proper by now. If I stepped outside, or moved aside the curtains, I would see it.

'Yeah?'

'Go to bed.'

'You too,' I tell him. To our own beds. Our separate rooms.

'I'll clean up a bit first.'

'Right then,' I say, and his timing is exactly right, as usual, for the glow of the Jarrowbrew has faded, and I have no energy for doing the tasks of a tomorrow that has already become today.

'TWO MORE PIES, one with mash, one with chips,' I tell Isley, through the hatch.

It's my job to be out the front, pulling the pints, listening to the conversations. The talk is always the same and forever mutating, growing to fit the crowd that listens. It might start with one deer, spotted on the moor, and then it becomes a magnificent stag, the biggest ever seen in these parts. More ears engage, and then it's two stags, and by the end of the week Bill is telling everyone *I was close enough to see their nostrils flaring* and I wonder where he'll go from there. Will he ever touch one, in his growing story? Will a stag come and eat from the palm of his hand?

They're laughing again, as Isley starts preparing the order. He was reluctant to cook tonight. Perhaps it's a reaction to what happened last week. *I don't want* him *touching my meal* said one of the farmers from the next village along, passing through on trade, and everyone at Bill's table stood up and stared him down, in silence, until he left.

We'll have none of that here, said Bill. They're a good bunch.

'Hey,' says Isley, through the hatch. 'Pies.'

There's laughter from the bar again. The stories are coming thick and fast tonight. They are inching and evolving around me.

'COME OUT AND sing with us!' shouts Bill Sedley through the serving hatch, after they've eaten and drunk, and drunk again. They've been singing "Harmless Molly" for what feels like hours, and I know Isley hates the arguments they have about which version is the right version, and the ensuing cacophony they create, but he comes out to a cheer and accepts their claps on the back with good grace.

They are allowed to touch him.

Still, I smile along as they launch once more into the story of a man who must leave his love to go to sea and fight the Spanish, and Isley joins in with his clear, cool voice. He's a wonderful singer. The locals don't know it, but that comes from the Qitan language, which is itself a song, beautiful to listen to. Preferable to the ruination of "Harmless Molly."

'You're a good lad,' says Steve Purley, at the end. 'Isn't he? He's a good lad. Fits right in.'

There's a high compliment indeed.

'Time, gentleman!' I call, and they complain, but it's good-natured moaning as they make for the door.

'TELL ME ABOUT growing up with your brother,' says Isley, when the last of them has gone. He's poured out two glasses of the standard brew for us, the one he makes by the gallon in the cellar, leaving the good stuff under the counter tonight. I don't mind. Not every night can be bathed and put to bed in the best memories.

'Why do you want to hear about Dominic?'

'He's a powerful man and I need friends.'

'You have me,' I tell him. 'Cosying up to a local official won't do you much good, anyway. He can't change anything. All he wants is to look responsible for it.'

'Was he always that way? Keen to…take responsibility?'

I shake my head. I don't talk about the here and now on Jarrowbrew, even the weak stuff. I don't talk about childhood, either. Nothing before Qita, and nothing after.

'Don't they say that the oldest sibling is keen to take responsibility?' Isley persists. 'They can be the bossy one.'

'How do you know what siblings can be like? I thought Qitans didn't have any.'

'Who told you that?'

'You did.' I can't be certain. Maybe I simply assumed it. Qitans have always seemed so separate to me: islands of their own. 'Or maybe it was Coach.'

He considers this, then says, quietly, 'I've got many siblings.'

This is new information, and I find that not only do I not want to talk about my family: I also don't want him to talk about his. The ties and losses on both sides. I thought we had an agreement not to even start down this path. The Skyward is the place where we can be alone, together. I don't want the past beyond our own timeframe to intrude. 'Let's drink to coolness,' I say, quickly, and we clink our glasses together, and drink it down. That will put an end to this line of conversation.

I have to conjure up a memory of Qita, quick, if I want that, so I say, 'This batch isn't a patch on the stuff in Langzin Square, is it?'

'Isn't it?'

*

So I tell him again about market time.

We were both there, but in different times, from different angles. I speak of it the way I remember it, mingled with the way it was told; the rules were explained to me before I arrived because it was not the kind of place one could understand simply by looking and listening. It made no sense unless you knew how to see it, make sense of it. So I came with foreknowledge through Coach.

Coach was the device implanted in my head by the Coalition, providing for all my information and entertainment needs—how did Coach already know about Qitan life, I wonder? Qitan workers on the base? I had Coach removed years ago, at the end of my contract, but it has left its ghosts. Sometimes I still ask a question to it, expecting an immediate answer to pop into my brain. Living that way can be addictive. I think maybe it's why I hate questions so much now. My thoughts need to be my own. Mine, and in the wake of Jarrowbrew, as I talk to you of our past, yours.

A high stone wall surrounds the square, in the centre of a bustling town. Traders queue at the start of each day to receive identical rectangular slabs from the market keeper. They're cut from the same stone as the walls; each one has a supple, shiny strap attached to one side, hung around the neck to balance the slab on the chest, creating a ledge upon which items for sale can be placed.

When all the slabs are taken, the keeper takes up a weighty metal cylinder and swings it in a circle overhead. The loud peal of a bell pours forth. The traders are then admitted, and they walk clockwise inside the walls, while prospective buyers sit on the central benches, in the shade thrown by the central cluster of fruiting trees.

The small surface area of each trader's ledge means that Jarrowbrew is the most popular product to sell. A tall, transparent container is placed in the centre with glasses around it, in a design said to mirror the market itself. Often Jarrowbrew has colour or flavour added to it, and the glasses may be individually decorated. The displays can be elaborate and ingenious, but does that mean the brew is better? Not necessarily, but then, this is all moot—at least in ways that I, a human, an outsider, can understand. The most inexplicable part to me is that no money changes hands. Locals insisted trade is the concept that explains Langzin Square best, but this is not supply and demand: when the glasses have all been used and the container is empty, the trader must leave. It does a trader no good to offer a more or less popular product—not that they strictly *offer* it at all.

On the day I visited, I was prepared. I did not

approach the traders, which would have been considered impertinent. I sat, in a shaded spot, and waited for one to come to me.

It took an age, and I felt so many eyes upon me. It was their chance to, at the very least, humiliate me. For what I was, for what I represented. But then a trader came to me, and said the words I had been hoping to hear. He spoke in his own language, then in Chinese, which I translated to English:

I give if you take.

He was tall, and his chin was even bigger than the usual, probably from years of wearing the strap upon it. His Jarrowbrew was plain, his glasses small and undecorated. The Qitan on my left shifted and tilted his head; I supposed jealousy on his part. I guessed this trader was well respected.

What made him trade with me? To learn his classic phrase in other languages, for just such a moment? What could I give him in return?

To trade is the choice of the trader, not the necessity, in Langzin Square. It is the business of hunting, by their own criteria. Do they look for those who seem in most need of their product? Or those who might reciprocate one day? That, it seems, is their decision to make.

I replied.

I am yours and you are mine.

A glass was poured, and given. I drank down the brew, and dreamed of a better Earth.

I don't think I'll ever taste anything as good again. But sometimes, Isley, sometimes, after a long night on my feet, and the thought of my son's disinterest in me biting, your best stuff comes close.

I stop talking.

'You know,' says Isley. 'That's not strictly accurate. About the ledges.'

'What bit?'

'The traders are meant to leave the market when they're sold out. But here's the thing—they have accomplices. Helpers have worked outside the walls to make very small tunnels, slanted downwards, through which Jarrowbrew can be poured. They wait outside and at a set time a trader stops by their hole, and refills their flask. Everyone knows it, and it is tolerated. It's... amusing, isn't it? We all think so.'

I picture the traders, surreptitiously putting their flasks to the walls at their designated spots, filling up once more. I had missed that entirely when I was there, although I had watched them for hours. But then, I wasn't looking for it.

'It's funny,' I say, 'how you can learn the rules of a place, but not which rules are okay to break.'

'You couldn't have broken them. It wasn't your place.'

I wonder if Isley is aware of the double meaning of what he just said.

'If everyone's been busy making holes for generations, doesn't that mean the walls are weakened?'

'Of course. The square is in danger of collapsing. Last thing I heard, the Coalition awarded a grant to try to repair the "damage". A report concluded that some unknown burrowing creature had attacked the structure.' He laughs, and I laugh and how ridiculous everything seems, right now, in the way our two sides of information have just come together.

'Who told you that?' I ask. 'About the Coalition?' Outside news can be very hard to come by in the Western Protectorate.

'Go to bed, Jem,' he says, and takes away the glasses to wash them up.

I WAKE, AND for a moment I don't know what I've heard. Then I place it—the squeak of the hinge of my bedroom door—and I know he's pushed it open, just a little.

'You okay?' I ask the darkness, in his direction.

'I did knock.'

'It's fine.'

'Can I come in for a minute?' Isley says, low and soft.

'Yeah. Come in.' He moves towards me, leaving the door open, and sits beside my hip, on the edge of my single bed. He's no more than a shape in the night. I sit up on my elbows, lean towards him. He has always been very clear that there can be nothing physical between us, but I've imagined moments like this: the possibility of this. Finding a way to be compatible.

'I have to tell you something,' he whispers.

What kind of things belong to this moment, between dreams and daily schedules? Am I hoping for certain words?

'Okay,' I say, taking his tone, matching the mood.

'I would ask you if you can keep a secret, but I know you can. You do. Keep your own secrets, I mean. Now I need you to keep one of mine. Is that all right?'

'It's fine.'

'There was an accident.'

But his voice is so casual. I push myself upright and lean back against the iron bedstead, icy through my thin pyjama top. My eyes are beginning to adjust to the darkness; he's still dressed in last night's clothes—the surfing tee-shirt, the loose trousers. He smells of the bar, and his curly hair hangs loose in those natural thick ringlets, around that large, curved chin. I can't focus on anything else.

I touch one of the ringlets. It's coarse and slippery. I hear his breathing.

It's so easy to touch him. I should have reached out years ago. His words are trickling through me. What did he say? There was an accident. Finally, I feel myself coming around to wakefulness, to possibility. To fear.

'Is it Fosse?' Please, not Fosse, not my son.

'No, no, it's me.'

'You're hurt?' The thought of that is unbearable. Don't let there be damage, not to him, to us.

'No, I just mean—it's here. Nothing to do with your kind.' Does he mean my family? Or my species? 'Can you come downstairs? I can't do this here. You'll want to get dressed.' He stands up and walks out, leaving the door ajar, and I dress with that crack in the door taking up all my attention, as if something unbidden might put its ugly eye to it, or slip through, if I'm not careful. I must guard against such disasters. I dress in my woollen jumper and loose jeans, over my pyjamas, then put on thick socks to keep out the cold of the stone floor. And only then do I dare to widen that crack in the door, and follow him down the stairs.

HE HAS LIT all the candles, snug in old wine bottles on the tables, and the fire is burning low. Isley is sitting at the small table nearest the fireplace, and he is looking at me.

'What is it?' I whisper.

He shifts in his seat, just a little, to one side, and only then do I realise that he's not alone.

A man sits opposite him. Or a woman. A Qitan. I should have seen it straight away: the thick jawline, the tiny nose. Blue blush to the skin. Another Qitan, here. She turns to look at me, features alive in the glow of the embers. The voice is high and light when she says, 'I'm so sorry, I don't mean to be difficult.' The meaning of the words as much as the tone makes me evaluate her as female. Crazy human assumptions.

'How are you here?' I ask.

'I can't get back.'

'You came by ship? How could a ship get through the Kissing Gate without being spotted?'

'It's very small,' says Isley. 'It's the suit. It's broken now. Something went wrong.' He gestures to what she's wearing; it's an orange one-piece outfit, resembling a boiler suit—worker's clothes.

'The suit is a spaceship?'

'Jem, this is Won.'

'One,' I repeat.

'Won,' he says again, drawing out the vowel.

'You really can't be here,' I tell her.

'I know. It's a difficult situation. It's not by choice,' she says. Her English is as good as Isley's.

'Can we fix your suit?' There have been incidents in other villages. Attacks. And there are villages we don't deal with, now, out of principle, like Simonscombe. Dominic made the case for breaking off communications with them, gave a speech at an open meeting when we heard about the burnings. He talked passionately of how we couldn't condone a return to barbarity.

They're not human, said Trevor, mildly, after raising his hand, *and I get my feed from there*. Dominic said, as if talking to a child: *They're not human, but we are, aren't we?* A few people clapped. It's a balancing act, a seesaw of beliefs kept in check only by fear of public disapproval, and I was concerned once I realised that; worried for Isley. But everything settled back down. This could shatter the peace.

'I don't think it can be fixed straight away. Not without getting a…' She stops speaking. There's a brief silence.

'Starter motor,' says Isley. 'That's the nearest way to describe it.'

'Qitan tech? How are you going to get that?'

'I don't know,' says Won. She puts her hand to her forehead, swipes at her hairline. It's a very familiar gesture, speaking eloquently of weariness. 'If I can get a message out, perhaps.'

'Right. A message.' It makes no sense to me.

'But for now,' says Isley, 'You'll hide, yes? Down in the cellar. That's the safest place.'

'Did anyone see her land?' The use of the pronoun slips out of me. Neither of them seems bothered by it.

'No, it travels without light, without sound. Nobody has noticed anything before.'

'Before?' I ask, and then I realise this is not a freak event. This is an error in a regular occurrence, and—yes—they know each other well. They finish each other's sentences, even. There's a level of communication between them that I'm only just beginning to see.

'Could we discuss this tomorrow?' says Won. 'I'm very tired.'

'We'll show you the cellar. We can make it comfortable.' He looks expectantly at me.

'That's why you woke me? To fetch bedding?'

'I didn't want you getting a shock. Finding Won here. Not without explanation.'

'Seems to me you haven't explained anything,' I say, and I'm angry. I don't want to be, but it can't be kept down, and I won't sleep now; he's robbed me of that as well. She's not meant to be here. I'll lie in bed for the rest of the night thinking about it.

'Could we talk more about it tomorrow?' he says.

'We could.'

'Then we will.' There's that hint of humour to his voice. At least, that's how I think of it. Or possibly it's a liking for completeness. For having the last word. He always does have the last word. But at least this time he doesn't tell me to go to bed.

They get up from their chairs and leave the room together. He follows her. She doesn't know the way, but he follows her, which makes no sense to me, and didn't they leave the room in some sort of synchronicity? Their steps in time? It reminds me of what some of the peacekeepers used to say, once they'd had a few too many at the Friday night functions. They'd talk of the way that Qitans could move as one, sometimes, without speaking. Of their mass migrations from one settlement to another. *They never put up a fight, but they could have slaughtered us,* one would say, and the others would agree. *Why just move over and let us take it?*

No battle. No military. Not one voice raised—at least, not theirs. A society of perfect peace. And now the ships of Earth come and go, taking their resources, selling their wealth, when they could simply have moved with one mind, and overwhelmed us.

Us and them.

All it took was the arrival of one more Qitan and I've begun to separate this situation into sides. How human I am, no matter how hard I try. We residents of the Western Protectorate, setting up our boundaries, priding ourselves on not being barbaric compared to the tiny villages not a few miles away. Being human is the problem, the whole huge problem in a nutshell, and I turn it over all night in my mind, sitting in the chair closest to the fire, stoking it and feeding it because the only alternative is the cold.

PART TWO

VALLEY FARM, FORGOTTEN, was a forty-minute walk from his school, in a straight line leading away from the morning sun, away from people, into the wilder and thicker territory of knotted trees on moorland.

Fosse was the boy with a taste for the places that had been bought up and left behind.

Broken slabs of old stone, long since laid, served as a crossing point for the stream. It dreamed of being a river after rainfall, but never quite managed to swell itself to such grandeur, and remained easily crossed even after the wet weather of the past week. Beyond that was a dank copse that smelled ever-pungent. Fosse breathed it in deeply as he walked—that smell of growing in the shadows—then erupted out into the sloping fields and took them at speed, legs pumping, across and down at a diagonal, into the valley.

Once there—then what? The bliss of empty, forgotten buildings. No plans, no people. No political machinations from his uncle who was tall and dry, like cut wheat, divorced from thriving life, choosing to see it as a negotiation of values. *Give and take. If you tidy your room, I'll make pancakes.* It was difficult to think of his uncle growing up years ago with his mother, who was messy with emotion; it spilled over into her voice whenever she tried to talk. *I hope you're okay*, she'd say to him, *you know, I really want you to be happy.* He would not go to Skyward Inn if he could help it.

Fosse did not want to become like his mother, or his uncle. The thought of it brought out fear in him, that it was a circle, a self-fulfilling prophecy, to become that which you hate because you hate it. So he tried not to think about it much, and was unsuccessful in that, too.

He already knew he was not strong, not in the way he thought a man should be strong. He had ideas of what he should become, but the body would not obey. It wanted to run, feel itself at work, at play. It erupted in hair and fluid. Lately, in the large barn that housed the rusted remains of machinery, it demanded he take off his trousers and stroke himself to a state of full arousal. He would then spill semen on the ground, and afterwards feel elated. It was the only kind of exchange he craved—to give of himself for this solitude, and he felt this forgotten covered ground was grateful, and accepting of his offering. Only later, when he returned home, was there the sudden heat of shame, when he saw his uncle once more. Uncle Dominic was so contained, bottled. Undiluted.

But there was no shame yet today.

Fosse stood in the barn, naked from the waist down, his trousers and boxer shorts folded carefully and placed on the seat of the rusted tractor, his shoes and socks laid before it. This was the only place where he was tidy.

Still in the flush of orgasm, he was pleased with the day. Forty minutes away, back towards the sun, his class was learning geography. The Earth is a tiny ball that is placed amongst other balls. It is round and there are dots upon its surface where people cluster, sometimes into megacities where the dots are too numerous to count, and there are barriers that protect the cities from climate disasters now, and machines that collect gases. The Kissing Gate was discovered fifteen years ago. The Coalition used the gate to travel to Qita, but the Western Protectorate disagreed with this action, and with the use of technology inside people's heads, and separated themselves from the rest of the world.

Geography was taught every day, and some days he ended up running from it. It was rammed into them so that nobody from outside the Protectorate could say *these children know nothing, they have been cut off from knowledge and now they're useless too.* His uncle had told him of the dangers of this view. But nobody ever made the journey to say such things to them, and if they said it elsewhere, to each other over computers and screens and internal chips, what did it matter to him?

His good humour, born from orgasm, faded. He wanted to kill something.

He took off his good watch with the loose strap and laid it upon his folded trousers, then retrieved the axe from the wall of the barn, held its curved handle of red wood, and lifted it up above his head. His knitted jumper rode his thighs, and cooler air found him, sneaked its fingers under the material. Yes, he wanted to kill an imaginary animal of vast size, like a creature from a book or from his own head. He could create his own vast, swamping monsters at times. He wanted to strike them all down dead.

He left the barn, wielding his axe.

Past the farmhouse with windows opaque from dust, then past the sheds made of corrugated iron sheets, the ribs red with rust. The boundary of the farm was marked by a long barbed wire fence, straddled by a wooden stile. Fosse climbed over and hopped down on to the lowest field. It was a patch of wetter grassland, tufted, sunken in places, never touched by strong sunlight.

He liked to feel the loose muddy ground surge up and around his toes, and imagine it rising from a deep cool place that the world shared. There could be no secrets or dissensions within that ooze, and he walked in it for a while, seeing his own footprints reincorporating, becoming only mud again, as he crossed his tracks.

He headed for the tree.

The tree bore many marks of the axe, but he was careful to never hit it deep in the same place twice. He had a fear of severing some part of it, even a small branch, although sometimes his murderous instinct sang out to do just that. But no, he wanted it intact, bearing the whacks of axe. He squared his shoulders, swung back, and landed a good blow. It felt strong. His back and chest felt a fine impact, vibrating through him. It was a good day, with each swing landing well, and for a while he imagined the trunk as the torso of his uncle, blood squirting from the wounds.

Fosse stopped chopping and saw he had cut too deep in one spot. The tree was creating thick orange sap that disturbed him. He stepped back, and remembered he had to return to the other life he lived.

And so he had reached the time to think about consequences. He would get into mild trouble for deserting school, as usual, but as long as he kept his absences to less than once a fortnight the adults had given up on punishment, choosing to sigh and see it as a symptom of Protectorate life. Other children helped parents on the farms, or got called to help on market days. His own absences were viewed in the same light. Only his uncle took offence to it, thinking his family somehow above that life, although he would have denied viewing it in such terms, even under torture.

Admit it. You think yourself superior.
No! No! We're all the same, working as equals to establish—arghhhhhhhh *screams*

He smiled at his own mental dramatics. But it was not anger at his uncle, not really. He understood it as a kind of general rage that liked to choose a face, and his uncle's face was the one he knew best. He pulled his thoughts away deliberately and pictured, instead, one of the monsters from his books, then cried, 'Take that!' He swung at the air until sweat had leapt from his pores and soaked him through.

His return could not be delayed any longer.

He began the trudge back across the field, through

the mud that no longer felt good underfoot. Back in the largest barn, he replaced the axe on the wall. He wiped his feet on the lip of the step up to the driver's seat of the abandoned tractor, then put on his clothes and watch with slow care.

When he emerged, a man called out to him. The man had not been there before—in the shadow of the barn—and he did not have a familiar face from anywhere. This was a stranger in a place that did not have strangers.

'Oy.'

Fosse jerked back his head and stared at the man, who was tall and thin and bald, wearing a bright blue shiny coat that reached to his knees. Two women flanked him, both of them smiling conspiratorially, as if in sympathy with themselves and nobody else.

'I saw you in my field,' said the man. 'Chopping at the tree.'

It wasn't his field, and Fosse knew it, but words never would come to him in front of other people.

'You've put your trousers back on, then.'

'It's not your farm,' said Fosse, surprising himself.

'It is now. I've taken it over. Get along, little one.'

One of the women laughed, the prettier one, and the boy ran away from their noise. But he could not escape their meaning. They had been watching him, had measured him in his size and activities, and found him lacking. He hated the idea of himself at the farm from that moment on and by the time he had reached the school he had decided to never go back there again.

It did not occur to him to tell anyone of their meeting.

'HOW'S HE GETTING on?' I ask. It says something that talking about Fosse is an easier option than having the conversation I came here to have.

'He still skips a lot of school. I've given up asking him about it.'

'I don't believe that for a second. You've never given up asking, whether someone's answering or not.' It was meant to be a mild joke but somehow it becomes accusatory and I immediately want to say *I'm sorry— that's not what I meant at all.* But it's too late and he wouldn't believe an apology anyway, not coming from me, so I watch him wince and hope the moment passes quickly.

We face each other over the kitchen table. The sink contains dirty plates and I keep catching the smell of last night's dinner, which was something meaty, possibly lamb. But that's the only thing out of place; everything else is washed, or cleaned. There's a neat stack of papers on one of the counters and a chalk board on the wall upon which Dom has written in bold, even letters:

FOSSE JOB W/C 27 SEP
WASHING AND DRYING DISHES

For once, his optimism for my son doesn't grate on me.

'Maybe you should talk to him instead,' Dom says, and I'm relieved at all the retaliatory barbs he didn't make. We know how to hurt each other if we're in the mood. Perhaps that's what brothers and sisters are, beyond the blood link: people who are too similar to feel predisposed to let any bullshit slide without a dose of perspective.

'You know he doesn't even want to be in a room with me.'

'Can you blame him?'

'I don't blame him for anything. Not even for skipping school. I did the same. Is Mr Rice still teaching geography?'

'He keeps promising to retire but at the start of each term he turns back up. And it's not like there's a queue of people waiting to take his place.'

Along with his duties as the head of the council, Dom is also a school governor. His commitment to the structures of the Protectorate amazes and amuses me; how is it possible to care so much for something that's obviously not working as it should? People can't get the medical care they need, steal from their neighbours or trade illegally with the boats that come from Swansea, and he claims we're all working towards a better future. But that's our upbringing. Our parents *believed* in it—they were the generation that set the separation in motion—and as far as I know they still do. Dom always did think they knew best because they were adults. Now he considers himself an adult and believes his own bullshit.

I wonder if Mum and Dad continue to tell him that separation was the correct course of action. They must, to justify their choices since then—the decision to relocate to Langleigh island, four miles off the coast, for instance. The place is populated by the rich and elderly who remain certain that all progress is bad progress. Except for the food and wine they import on their own terms, of course. Dom visits them once or twice a year. He always asks me to come along, even though I haven't gone with him since my first year back from Qita.

The idea of him just giving up on someone—who does he think he's kidding? That's why I left my son in his care.

'I brought biscuits,' I say. 'Ginger nuts.'

I have a packet that Andy Pocock traded for a drink last night; Isley told me to keep it for myself. Nothing sweet agrees with him. I take the biscuits from my bag and put them on the table. The bright lettering on the orange background is an eye-catching shock.

'Christ,' he says, unexpectedly.

'Shall I open them?'

He pauses, then shakes his head. 'I'd feel bad about it, without Fosse here. He'll want one.'

'I wasn't going to eat them all right now!'

'Aren't they a gift?' he says. 'I thought that meant you don't get to eat any of them.'

'Fine. Whatever. What time will he get home, then?' I already know the answer to this question, having timed my appearance to catch him. He should be here in twenty minutes, leaving me enough time to see him with a good excuse for leaving soon afterwards, with the evening drawing in.

Dom checks his watch. 'Actually, I should get going. There's a council meeting at the Schilling barn. Fosse is meant to meet me there. I've enlisted him as secretary this year.'

'I bet he's loving that.'

'He hasn't complained. Do you want to come along? It's enough of a walk to give you time to work up the courage to say whatever it is you want to say. I just need to change my clothes—you okay to hang here for a minute?'

'I'm not the one on a schedule,' I call after him as he leaves the room, and I hear his feet on the stairs and the closing of the bedroom door. I can picture the room he's standing in, even though my remembrance of it is eighteen years out of date. Back then it was my parents' room, and that meant it was dominated by my mother's taste: a white dressing table with pink and blue scarves draped around the oval mirror; a matching wardrobe with thin gold handles; a large bed with its foot at the window to give an unimpeded view over the housing estate trailing down the hill, to St Luke's church, and the graveyard. The land around this house had once been only trees, when it had been the property of my mother's family, but the wealth was mishandled generations back and the ground sold off to a developer. My mother never seemed to mind. She liked the addition of neighbours to her view; she had loved to lie in bed in the morning, curtains thrown back, and look over them all, noting at what times light switches were turned on and off, and cars moved.

The last time I visited the island, she was watching the birds on the feeders through the windows of the residential lounge in much the same spirit. She could make companions from anything, as long as she read no threat in it. And my father sat quietly beside her, not needing to speak or act on her behalf at that moment. I wondered if that was peace, to him: a land without light switches and cars.

I'm tempted to climb the stairs and open the door, just to see what's changed up there. The decor, and the view.

Are those slender gold handles still in place? How many houses on the estate stand empty now? How many birds can we observe in flight today?

I take my cup to the sink, pour away the remains of the mint tea, and turn on the tap. Running water is maintained by the water board as long as we pay them in milk and produce, which they can market as Westward-Protectorate-certified. I only know this because Dom was involved in arranging the deal and he told me about it, back when we used to talk to each other.

I wash up my cup and the dishes. It's a small gift to a boy from his mother.

'RIGHT, SPIT IT out.'

We walk along, side by side, down the back lanes leading to the Schilling barn. The hedgerows are overgrown and vibrant, blackbirds are singing, and there's no traffic and nobody to hate for miles. To many parts of the universe, this would be a form of heaven. They make romantic films, out there in the world, set in the Protectorate. Or they used to. I used to watch them via Coach when I was between assignments on Qita. I missed the Protectorate, then, even though nothing in the films was accurate. It felt almost like home.

But I've been back for so long that it's become

impossible to appreciate the place, even for a moment. I'm ungrateful for all I have every single day. For some reason I think of Isley, and I feel worse.

Here goes. Here goes this conversation.

'I don't want to upset you, okay? That's really not my goal.'

'Great start,' says Dom.

'A situation has come up at the inn and I can't solve it by myself. I need your help. You're not going to like it, but I need you to be my brother and not the head of the council.'

He's looking ahead, up the lane. I sneak a glance at his face. He's tense. He's so easy to read, so I know I've said the wrong thing already. 'I'm both of those things, Jemima,' he says. 'They're not separate.'

'No, I know. I understand that.'

'Is it Isley? He's in trouble?'

It's so unusual to hear Dom admit to Isley's existence that I forget the words I've decided to use. He approved Isley's application to come with me and reopen the Skyward, but I think he's regretted doing that ever since, and he has as little to do with him, and with Jarrowbrew, as possible. But the brew has been a huge success, and some would argue that the Skyward has become the heart of this area. It's always busy, always happy. We work hard to make it so.

What was I going to say? There was something about helping those who fall on difficult circumstances and everybody being determined to solve the problem as soon as they can and be on their way, but I can't form it into a sensible order. 'So it turns out Isley has a friend,' I say, and a sour note creeps into my voice. I swallow, and go on. 'A Qitan friend who's been coming in to drop off—things. Supplies.'

He's silent.

'She has a really small vehicle. It's like a suit that she wears. I've not seen anything like it before. But something went wrong and it crashed, and now she needs a specific part to mend it.' I take the paper from my pocket and hold it out to him. He stops walking and stares at it. Won drew the part she needs upon it; it's very complex, with lots of tiny marks and lines. Underneath it she wrote something in Qitan, then something in Chinese, and then the English words:

STARTER MOTOR

'Starter motor?' He says, then laughs. 'Is this a joke?'
'Absolutely not.'
'How the hell do you want me to get a starter motor for a Qitan spacesuit? This kind of stuff doesn't exist anyway. Qitans don't have that sort of tech. You know that.'

'All I can tell you is what I saw.'

'So where did she get it from? And what supplies is she dropping off?'

I really don't want to get into this. He's always treated Jarrowbrew with suspicion, and this would only confirm his worst theories. He'd be right, right about me reopening the inn and drinking with Isley and the addictive quality of it all, and more than anything I don't want him to be right about me, even if he is. 'I think it would be better if you don't know the details, wouldn't it? I mean—we just get the part, she mends the thing, she's gone. Nobody knows anything.'

'I know. And I get the part, somehow. How were you thinking I'd manage it? Through my connections, like what I do is some sort of seedy operation? And I trade— what? Fruit? Vegetables? Other people's hard work?'

'Isley said he'll pay for it.'

'In what?'

'Isn't it in everybody's best interests to have her gone?'

He considers this. Perhaps he's thinking about the burnings in Simonscombe. We have only our imagination to tell us what that looked like, how things went wrong, but I know we share a powerful mind for dark fantasy. We played political games of war and murder as children, with countries and people conflated, stolen and shaped from communal memories that passed down the line. *You be a Nazi and I'll be Great Britain.* So he can imagine what has happened there, what might happen here, and which side he needs to be on to stop it.

He folds up the paper, puts it in his coat pocket, and we walk on, at speed. It feels like a competition to keep pace.

The lane curves left, and the Schilling barn comes into view up ahead. It's not exactly a barn at all, but the largest building for miles, built as a community centre and music hall on money from the Coalition decades ago, offering classes and experiences for the community. It's been falling down a piece at a time ever since. The roof is the biggest of its problems at the moment; I can see the darker patches of rain damage from here.

I hear myself say, 'What are you thinking?'

'I'm thinking that something like this was always going to happen and I should have known you'd be involved in it.' He sighs. 'I don't know, okay? I don't know what to think.'

'But could you—?'

'What, I have to make a decision right now? Right at this moment? I'll think about it, all right?'

'Yeah, of course.'

'Come see Fosse. Try not to upset him. I'll think about it.'

I have to take his barbs because I've asked him for something. That's how it works. I have to shut up and listen to his insinuations that I only upset my son with my occasional presence. So I only tell myself, in my head, in time to my footsteps, that Dom can go fuck himself.

'I should say,' Dom continues, 'Bob died. Bob Satterly. The funeral was a couple of days ago.'

Bob babysat us once or twice. He's vivid in my head upon the mention of his name, alive and laughing, attempting to show me how to knit without much success. 'What did he die of?'

'Cancer. He'd been ill for a year or so. We got him some treatment on a deal. Chemotherapy, at Bristol. But it didn't work.'

'You should have told me!'

'I'm telling you now. I didn't think it would matter to you. You haven't seen him in years, have you? Too busy at the inn.'

And I have to take that too.

We reach our destination, and find we're the first to arrive because of the ferocious pace at which we've walked. Dom says, 'We might as well try to do something about the roof, then. I think there's a ladder round the back,' and I go hunting for it, at his command, because that's what sisters who need a favour from their brothers do.

* * *

DOM POUNDS ANOTHER nail into the tile, but he's no roofer. We're working on the principle that any repair is better than none.

Still, the rhythm is a beating heart between us as I hold the tile in place, and when the job is done and we look up, together, there's Fosse in the distance. He walks along the edge of the field, heading for us, but his face pointed down to the earth so that only his long brown hair is visible. There's no point in waving.

We watch him, then look back at the tile.

'I think that's done, isn't it?' says Dom.

'I reckon.'

It's a beautiful view from up here, and the day is darkening on the edge of the horizon. The spire of St Luke's is visible, and the Skyward is up on the top moor, out of view, in the other direction. Dom slots the hammer in his belt and begins the journey back down the ladder. I follow him, wishing I could stay up here longer, but it must be nearly time for the meeting to start.

Years ago, I couldn't say how many, Bruno Schilling, who owned this barn, returned to the Cologne zone. I still think about him every now and again. He was a good councillor and a fine musician. He taught Dom about politics and then taught me to play the guitar, and he'd sit between our parents around the dinner table and make both of them laugh in different ways. He had an easy grace to him, a feeling of bonhomie, and a magnificent moustache. The West Country Music and Community Hall—to give it its proper name—was his pet project, but everyone knew it as the Schilling barn. He was always there, involved in one thing or another. He connected us all to each other. I miss that feeling, sometimes.

'Dom!' calls a voice from inside, and we walk through the double doors into the largest of the meeting rooms, with a vaulted ceiling and torn posters on the walls for things that happened an age ago. There's a strong smell of damp. How did I miss everyone arriving? But here they are, ready for their meeting. They must have reached the building while Dom hammered away.

Doctor Clarke gives me a nod, and quietly taps his watch. I'm overdue a check-up at the surgery, and he tries to keep us all in good working order; prevention is better than cure when any modern treatment involves intense trading with the Coalition. Illness is an expensive business. He turns back to his conversation with Reverend Sumner. She's quite new to the village. Dom chose her from thousands of applicants for the position of our spiritual leader, and he told me he did a good trade to get her. I don't know where she came from, and I don't want to find out. I have no interest in the church, but a lot of locals take comfort from her presence in St

Luke's, and I've heard good things about her, which turn into comments on her surprising youth and attractiveness after a few brews.

Benny Sykes, our village policeman, is in attendance too. He's wearing his off-duty clothes, thank goodness. I can't stand the sight of him in that ancient blue uniform with the hard, curved hat sticking up from his head, and even the truncheon at his side. He comes from generations of law enforcement officials, apparently, and he thinks it's his right to drink for free. There's not much we can do about it apart from keeping some specially watered-down stuff under the bar for when he shows up.

Freya Satterly is unwrapping cling film from a large plate of sandwiches set on a trestle table. Her dog is standing to attention beside her, displaying that eagle-eyed, avuncular quality unique to overfed Labradors. It's nothing like most of the dogs that come into the inn, on the heels of older owners: wiry Collies or terriers that look keen to plunge into rabbit holes or snap at badgers, and shouldn't be touched.

I feel my nerves kick in. What's the right thing to say to a grieving wife? I can't believe Dom didn't tell me she'd be here.

'Fosse will help you eat those,' says Dom.

'Just so long as I don't have to take any home,' says Freya. 'I've got piles of it. Most of it will have to go in the bin. I've no idea why I made so much food, like I was expecting the five thousand to turn up. Hello Jemima! How lovely to see you!'

'Hi,' I say, and in a rush, 'I'm so sorry about Bob, I've only just heard, or I would have come and said it sooner.'

'He knew you wished him well. It was a good wake you missed. We decided not to have it at the inn, as we weren't exactly regulars, were we? It just didn't make sense.'

'Of course.'

'It was only a get-together at our house.'

Dom nods, slowly and sincerely. 'Bob would have wanted it that way. Close friends only.' I make a mental note to kill him later for putting me in this position.

There had been something very warm about Bob, as I remember him. I want to say that, but the conversation has already moved on and that is, in itself, a form of relief. I stand there and listen to small talk for a while. There's been a good apple harvest this year. Everyone is sick of apple pies already.

After a few minutes Dom says, 'Let's get started, shall we? Jem, haven't you got to get back?'

'I—um, yeah, I should go. It was lovely to see you all.' As I reach the door, Fosse is just coming in. He looks up at me and I see a flicker of surprised annoyance cross his face. I'm not even worthy of real hatred; my presence irks him, no more, no less. But I've seen him, and that's enough. It has to be enough, because that's all there is between us, and Dom's right—that's my fault.

'Fancy a picnic some time?' I ask him, and he says, 'Yeah, great.'

'Okay! Great.'

'I have to...' He points to the gathering of the council. Of course, he's taking minutes. Then he walks past me, and I leave to return to the Skyward. Whatever they say about that place, they don't want me to be anywhere else.

FOSSE TOOK MINUTES. He had little interest in it. He didn't know what was important to those who spoke, and he disliked his own handwriting, which looked like the work of a boy.

He kept his eyes open for the moments when a change would come over the room; the usual business would give way to a surge of interest, and they would sit up and lean in, and their faces would become younger, more animated. At those times he drew a corresponding expression in the margin of the exercise book. Later, it would be his job to shrink his notes into bullet points of order, and his uncle would check it through before filing them in his study.

Meeting began.

Fosse drew a smiling face. They always started with smiles. They talked of trade, and the smiles were put away. The request box for the village was full to overflowing again, his uncle began—was the larger box on the way? That was one approach to needs and wants, Fosse thought. To make a bigger space to store them all rather than try to diminish the pile. But it seemed that the requests would always grow to fit the space, even if a box the size of a building was fitted on the green, with a slot wide enough for everyone to post their bodies through. Why waste time with slips of paper when everyone wanted everything?

Mrs Tildy promised to raise the issue with Mr Samuels, who had told her last month that he was making a bigger request box when he had time.

He drew two dots for eyes and a straight line of a mouth in the margin.

Mrs Satterly opened her crocheted bag and emptied the pile of request slips in the centre of the table, next to the sandwiches. The group began to sort them. It was not Fosse's job to list all the things written there. He only had to record any actionable events for the council, so he wrote:

Requests sorted and discussed.

—as he usually did at this point, and turned his thoughts fully inwards, to find the people at Valley Farm waiting there for him. A man and two women, standing together. The women hadn't looked similar, but they had stood together as if they were family, on either side of the man. They began to exert fear and fascination over him, easily, both feelings sprouting smoothly from the circumstance of the meeting. His nakedness from the waist down, his vulnerability, and the axe in his hands: they must have watched him, his regular patterns and private compulsions.

And the farm had been *his* place.

Now it belonged to them. He had rolled over and accepted it, the takeover completed with one statement.

In his thoughts he retrieved the axe from the wall of the barn and sank it deep into the man's neck, where it made the sweet, full sound of splintering wood. He found, in this fantasy, that he did not bear the man any ill will; but it would be necessary to kill him in order to make himself a serious object in their shared eyes. His land, his place. His marks on the barn and the tree and the body of the man.

His uncle was speaking of a request for more sanitary products to be stocked in market, his cheeks taking on colour, the others nodding with their eyes elsewhere. *Also more baby food*, his uncle said, *and we should prioritise this—or possibly arrange more support for the girls in school to learn about feeding infants from the foods we can grow ourselves, you know, natural alternatives.* Fosse's attention fixed on the phrase. He wanted to know about alternatives, wherever they existed, to everything. To life. He wrote:

Natural alternatives discussed.

He drew three circles in the margin: two open eyes and an open mouth of wonder.

But what of the man at the farm? Imagine being a traveller, a conqueror. To simply turn up on soil and stamp it as property. There was something very human about it. That was why he did not hate the man, he realised. They had recognised each other as human in that moment, and it was right for Fosse to be mocked and demoted, at least for now. For now.

Strawberries, his uncle was saying, *who on earth is requesting strawberries in October? The whole idea is to trade only for necessities and live within our means and in season as much as possible.*

Let them eat sprouts, said Reverend Sumner and Fosse wrote:

Reverend Sumner made a produce-based joke.

He drew another smiley face in the margin of the exercise book before turning over the page.

The requests went on.

His mother's presence had surprised him. She never did know what to say—a trait she had passed on to him, uniting and dividing them. But that was fine. He associated the inability to speak any real words with her utterly; he could not remember seeing her in any other state. Every time she saw him, she was all eyes and no mouth.

He wished he were old enough to go to the Skyward Inn one night and drink, but only if she was present as a mute witness to it, behind the bar, she in her element and he in his. He wanted to look at the Qitan she lived with in that place, see the two of them together when they thought nobody was looking, and understand why she chose to be there instead of in his house.

The requests were all sorted into *urgent, possible, not actionable*, and *declined*. Next there was Protectorate business, his uncle's area of expertise. He was the conduit of the Higher Council, bringing the big messages to the smaller people in swallowable sizes. Fosse concentrated on his uncle's feedback from the latest gathering, in Plymouth, and took notes.

Water and electricity tithes on track at agreed Coalition rates, but an increase forecast as from next quarter.

An outbreak of illness at St Ives = a quarantine being set up. Anyone arriving from that area without the proper documents should be checked and reported.

Tourism plans raised again. Electricity expansion offered in some smaller towns if a plan for "visitor villages" approved? A fixed amount of tourists per year to five "traditional working villages". Would this be possible?

He looked around the tables at the expressions and then drew three very angry faces in the margin, surrounded by lightning bolts. They talked on and on about the betrayal of the founding values and his uncle nodded and nodded. Nodding was a hugely important part of these meetings.

The Chairman indicated that he would feed back the Council's objections to the proposal.

Fosse was pleased with his choice of words. He was getting better at this. He supposed it was true, after all, that practice made perfect. He had doubted it, even as adults had repeated it as ineffable wisdom from some deep source that they all tapped into. The well of knowledge. He never seemed to run that deep or cold himself.

He considered finding another axe to practise killing strokes with, so that he would be ready to chop off the man's head when he came of the right age for such a challenge, but it was obvious to him that only the axe in the barn—the one with the curved red handle—would do. It had a way of fitting to his hand. He would fetch it and keep it. If the farm were no longer his, the axe at least would not be taken away.

'Did you get that, Fosse?'

Brought back to the room, to the words; everything was loud and bright and without sequence as if the last hour had run together. He shook his hand.

'Just to make a note that we're taking a family with farming experience from the immigration list.'

'*Is* that agreed?' said Doctor Clarke.

As they discussed it, Fosse wrote:

It was agreed to take one family with farming experience.

His uncle would win the argument. He was good at that. He was talking once more about the importance of bringing in new blood with old skills. It was one of his favourite phrases. *No links to the area*, Benny Sykes was saying, and the reply was familiar too: *the only people with the skills we need aren't from here. They've farmed in hot climates with little resources. They need to escape their deserts and we need people who can make less fertile soil yield results. The Valley Farm, for instance. They could try to make that profitable again.*

Fosse stopped writing.

His land was being taken from him yet again, this time in the public domain. And, beyond his resentment, there was another feeling—a compulsion to a different form of action. An obligation, as part of this community, to say something about the farm. Something only he knew.

He thought about it carefully.

First, he would get into trouble for going there, but that did not bother him much.

Second, he would be choosing a side. He was not interested in allegiance to his uncle or their way of life. Nor to protecting the man and the women, although he liked this knowledge he held of them, over them. He was the most informed person in the room, and that had never happened before.

He rejected the impetus to speak of it, and pushed the feeling deep down into the soft dark spot he kept inside. It could swallow difficult things and hold them, fast and unmoving. He had discovered the place soon after the return of his mother from the war, when she had decided to live in the inn. Since then it had been the most convenient of pockets.

The conversation turned to the idea of visiting the Valley farm to check its state before agreeing to the immigrants, and Fosse also poured that into his pocket without a qualm. The council never got around to doing anything, he thought. He couldn't imagine them gathering outside of this room. But he decided to fetch the axe sooner rather than later, just to be safe. He had to be ready to strike a killing blow before others got involved. His uncle, standing on the land telling the man and his women to go, was an image that made Fosse shrivel.

Then it was time for Any Other Business, and there were ongoing issues of broader scope that were regularly raised in this slot such as the state of the world outside and what his uncle knew of it. Fosse paid no attention because nothing would be revealed. The meeting drew to a close and the plate of sandwiches was pushed in front of him.

'Eat up,' said Freya, and her dog, Bailey, put his large heavy head on his knee, his eyes turned up to the lip of the plate, jutting over the edge of the table. The head was warm and substantial. Bailey's body was the most real thing he had felt since the axe striking the tree. He stroked the head and felt the muscles of his arm complain, remembering how the blow had jarred his bones, connecting the energy. He ate the sandwiches with the other hand. They were filled with the local cheese, which he did not care for since tasting a different cheese a few weeks ago. His uncle had called him into the kitchen by candlelight, late in the evening, and presented him with a wedge of something blue-veined. *Cheese from abroad*, his uncle had said, under his breath. It was a squashy, overpowering revelation of taste and smell. Since then the idea of cheese had been spoiled for Fosse. He wished he hadn't tasted something else to act as a comparison to what he had—or maybe it would have been all right if it had just been called a different name.

He ate the plate of sandwiches just the same, in the grip of disappointment at the taste, and Bailey disposed quietly of the harder crusts of bread, opening and closing his big mouth with surprising and patient delicacy. The dog seemed quite certain that there would be more crusts, even after the plate was empty. For a long time he stayed put, looking up, expecting something good to keep on coming.

*   *   *

THE EARLY EVENING hush could be mistaken for a failing business, if one didn't know the business. But the truth is that Skyward Inn is thriving, as I'd imagine only pubs can in times when others struggle. It lives on its own terms, after the sun has set. People come late and stay as long as they can, at the end of difficult days: a gift to themselves when nothing else is giving.

Isley used to talk a lot during this time, when we first reopened. He'd imagine where people were, and what they were doing. *I bet Bill Sedley is asleep in an armchair, storing up energy for drinking tonight. I bet he's snoring.* Isley is fascinated by snoring. *Benny Sykes is investigating an interesting case of a missing chicken.* He'd create alternative realities for them all, apart from the regulars who only leave when they are forced to. They tend to sink into the walls, and get forgotten about. They sit back from the light, at their favourite tables, like Geoff who is already three brews in today and humming to himself. He's an old man with all the old tunes in his head. And like Ailsa, who is taking her time, nursing her first. She traded a bar of chocolate for that. I have no idea where she might have got that from. Isley will use it to make chocolate chip muffins, and stick that on the menu. They'll do well, no doubt. It's going to be a busy night for us.

We've not talked about the menu yet. We've not really talked at all since Won arrived, not like we used to. And as for Won, she has not moved from the cellar. I set up some bedding down there, and loaned her some clothes. A shirt, some jeans. I've nodded to her when I've been down there, usually fetching something, and she has smiled back. One time I caught her pacing from end to end, her suit in her arms. As soon as she saw me, she sat down, on a barrel, crossing her legs. The smile took over her face and presented itself to me. It repulsed me with its rubbery quality. I couldn't manage to smile back.

Still, it won't be long. I have to believe that. Dom won't let me down. It's been three days since I asked him, and he's not responded, but he's reliable. That's what he wants to be.

I pick up one of the more dilute bottles of brew, because that's the kind of thing bar staff do. This is nothing like the stuff Isley keeps under the counter, just for us. I haven't touched Jarrowbrew since Won arrived, but I find I only want it when there's nothing to do. Come on, come on, the evening crowd. Tonight is darts night. The Away team is from Wivencombe, seven miles away. They'll be coming by horse and cart, and I'll hear the hoofbeats, then the clatter to a standstill outside. The door will be thrown back and there they'll be, demanding all I can pour, and pies for the finish.

The door opens.

But it's a slow squeak, with no force behind it, and a

woman that I'd guess is Hispanic in origin enters quietly, without fanfare. She closes the door behind her. I get a good look at her long waterproof coat and thick hiking boots with the laces looped many times. She carries an unwieldy concertina of paper, crunched into one hand.

'Hello,' she says, with a self-conscious air, and approaches the bar.

'You all right?' I ask her.

'I think maybe I'm lost. Is this Porlock?' She has a soft accent that I haven't heard before, not even on the base at Qita where many languages mingled.

'No, you're too far down the coast for that. Which direction have you come from?'

'From...' She puts down the map; it covers the bar easily. It's an Ordnance Survey map, years and years out of date—from before the separation. Some of the places don't really exist anymore, except in name. It's strange to see them laid out, jumbled shapes of differing sizes, as if the lines of their boundaries were solid. '...there.' She points to Lynton.

'You walked from Lynton?'

She nods.

'So you need to carry on for a bit longer, then. It's at least five miles. You won't make it tonight. Do you need a place to stay? We have rooms.'

'No, no, it's fine. Thank you.'

'I can do you a reasonable rate. We take trade.'

'I have an appointment tomorrow morning. Here.' Her finger slides along the map to rest in a fold. 'At five o'clock.'

'In the morning?'

'Yes. So do you.'

She doesn't look up; all I can see is the long straight line of her centre parting, and the fall of her hair down to the map. I look at the place she's now pointing at—it's much closer. Less than a mile away, on the clifftops, at Wreckers Cave. I used to walk there with my parents and Dom. Her fingernails are painted red. Who the hell has nail polish anymore?

'Dominic said you can come,' she says.

This is it. This is the trade, and it took me too long to work out what she means. I feel out of my depth. She glances up at me, under her eyelashes, and I see her amusement. Sweat springs up on my back and in my armpits, and I'm meant to be saying something easy, something casual, for the benefit of those who might be listening to this conversation, except that there's nobody listening, not even the regulars will be paying attention, and I feel like I'm acting in a drama with no audience and I've still managed to forget all the lines.

'Oh, right. I understand,' I say. 'Got it. That's fine. That's fine.'

'Bring the suit and the payment.'

'The suit…?'

'To check. That the part is right.'

There's a sound coming from stage left. Hoofbeats. They clatter to a halt outside and then, on cue, the door is flung back, and Barry Tarkold is standing there with his darts team behind him. He's big and meaty and likes to be the centre of attention; he's not above quoting Greek philosophers to win arguments, as if nothing could top a comment made over two thousand years ago. He likes me, I think. He often tips me with boiled sweets that seem to come from nowhere with a flourish.

'Miss Jemima Davey!' he calls, loud, and the woman with the map flinches. The rest of the team swerve around him as he stands in the doorway, and busy themselves with removing their coats.

'You're early,' I tell him. 'Our team's not even here yet.'

'We wanted time for a warm-up drink. Hello,' he says, 'What have you got there?' He comes up to the bar and leans over the woman, close. She tenses. 'Look at that! I haven't seen a map like that for an age. Might even be worth some money. I'd frame that.'

'Thank you,' she says. She folds it back up and steps away.

'You on a walking holiday?' he asks her, then turns to me. 'Best make it a round of brews, Jem.'

'No, I live here,' she tells him, which he knew, of course. There are no holidaymakers.

'Really? I've not seen you.' As if someone could know everyone in the Protectorate. But he feels like he owns it all, I suppose, and he's enjoying himself with this encounter. 'You lived here long? Go back generations, do you? No, seriously, you're an essential worker, then? Here on council leave?'

'Yes, I'm a building surveyor.'

He raises his eyebrows in a mockery of fascinated interest. 'Right. Essential.'

'Thank you,' she says again, and makes her way to the door. How small she is when surrounded by the darts team of Wivencombe.

'Don't get lost now,' one of them says to her, and the others laugh. She smiles along, and exits to their jollity. I concentrate on pouring the brews and fielding their comments, and soon the home team arrives to roars and posturing, and the match begins. The woman is forgotten. I pour brews and accept money when it's given. There are also apples and potatoes and a paper bag of broccoli, and a woman's wristwatch in lieu.

'Took that off your wife's dressing table? I'm sure she won't mind,' says Mike Treaven to Simon Lane, home team members, and everyone who knows Simon's wife laughs at the idea of her not minding.

I'm in the thick of it. The men ask me for drinks, and I pour them; they flirt with me and I flirt back, just a little, just enough. How do I know what enough is? I'm good at this, I enjoy it: noise, business, the *thunk* of the darts into the board like drumbeats calling me up, giving me music to which I can work. But all I can think of is the woman.

The match is over. The Away team have won and they're lording it over the local lads, of course, but that's the way the game is played, and everyone is cheerful. I head to the kitchen and find Isley finishing up the pork and apple pies, his shirt sleeves rolled back and his apron in place, tied in a double bow around his waist. He looks up and smiles at me as if I'm the only person he wants to see, and I remember why I asked him to come back here with me.

'It's ready,' he says. 'I'll dish it, you carry it through.'

'My brother found someone. The trade's on.' Is this really the right time? It doesn't matter; I need to tell him.

He looks at me, a tea towel in one hand and a fish slice in the other. 'That's good,' he says, cautiously.

'It's on for tomorrow morning. Early. Out by Wrecker's Cave. I'll go. Give me the stuff to trade and I'll take it.'

'I'll come with you.'

'No, it'll be fine, I think it's better—'

'I'll come with you,' he says. 'I should be able to tell if it's the right part.'

'Right.' I hadn't thought of that. He's worried about the part, not about me. I keep looking at him. I want him to say something real. Something about us.

'She needs to be on her way,' he says. 'And then...'

'Then things can get back to normal.'

'Yes. I've missed normal.'

I see a moment of recognition in his eyes and I remember, I remember him. 'Me too.'

There's a roar from the front and he says, 'You'd better start taking these out.' He plates up the first two pies and I take them up, and carry them through.

THE TWO TEAMS wear each other out early, and the Away lads leave a little after midnight.

'It's a long journey home on the old horse and cart,' Barry Tarkold says to me, 'unless you're going to offer me a bed here and keep me warm all night?' Everyone laughs.

The Home team stay a little longer, but soon run out of things to trade or promises to make. Christmas is on their minds, perhaps. They'll need to store up to make it special. Or maybe nobody's heart is quite in it because mine isn't. Usually I chivvy them along into staying longer and spending more than they should, but I didn't put up a fight when they reached for their coats. Sometimes I feel like I'm the vital organ that keeps life pumping around the inn. Isley too, of course; his blood flows through it too, and it pulses in time with his breaths. The inn is alive to us both. It is our baby.

I've never seen a Qitan baby, but I've seen Qitan blood.

'Are we there yet?' says Isley, like a child, and I try to remember how long it used to take to walk to Wrecker's Cave from the Skyward. Possibly an hour, but those times had been strolls, easy meanders so as to let the roast dinners settle. Back then the inn had been called the Lamb and Flag, and it had been famous for its Sunday carveries. The spread of food had been a fine sight that everyone took for granted. New Zealand lamb, I remember. No chance of that now. Tiramisu on the menu for dessert, or Black Forest gateau.

We're walking much faster than I ever walked after that large lunch, walking towards the sea through a rising veil of darkness, my torch beam shining on the broken, tufted grass, the sheep manure, the mud. The world is definitely getting lighter around us, and colder too—cold in this moment before a dawn, and crystal sharp, and alive with the rhythm of the sea.

'Another ten minutes,' I guess.

'We're going to a cave,' says Isley.

'There's an old way down to the beach from it. It was used for smuggling, but also wrecking. This was a famous wrecking spot, although there are others down the coast.'

'What are wreckers?' He keeps pace beside me, although he could easily go faster with his long legs.

'On stormy nights, men would stand on the edge of the cliff with a lantern, signalling to passing ships looking for safe harbour.'

'Really? That sounds kind.'

'They'd be leading the ship on to the rocks,' I tell him. 'There's no safe harbour, along this coast. Only rocks. And once the sailors were drowned and the ship broken up, the wreckers would go down to the shoreline and steal the cargo that had washed up.' I don't tell him that they'd also kill any sailors who survived the wreck. When I was young I had a book about a girl who had been born into a wrecking family; she turned into a heroine by defying them all and leading soldiers from the town to witness the dark deeds of her father and brothers one night. I could never tell if it was fiction or reality. It was illustrated in pen and ink, and the picture of the climactic scene has stayed with me—the Sergeant in his braided uniform and the girl pointing, the two of them in the background, while the twisted face of her father driving a shovel into the body of a sailor filled the bottom half of the page. The sailor's arms were thrown up, partially blocking a view of his contorted expression. Strange, how I was allowed such a gruesome story, and yet my parents viewed it as my heritage, no doubt. A tale of the West Country. They could be proud of anything, from scones to cathedrals, murders to Morris dancing, all of which had no relevance to the life they were living.

But perhaps I'm wrong. It could be that all these things are still relevant, even now. Even to me. Or moving back into relevance as we journey on. Religion, tradition, wreckers.

'The past is so dark here,' says Isley, and I turn off the torch to find I can see passably well. It's closer to dawn than I realised. I increase my pace, and Isley maintains his step beside me.

'FINALLY.'

I don't know this tall man, have never seen him before, but that one word is enough to tell me he's local. He stands at the cliff edge, and he holds a short metal rod with a pronged end. Is it a starter motor? I'm glad of Isley's presence, and his knowledge; I don't know what I'm doing. Between the two of us we might be able to make this work. The drop to the sea beyond—a bright shining wall now the sun is rising—is close but Isley is closer, sticking with me, and we have survived many things together, he and I. We have survived.

A woman emerges from the cave, combing her fingers through her hair. She's the woman who came to the inn earlier, but although she's in the same clothes, down to the laced walking boots, she is different. Relaxed. Two men follow her out, and their stance strikes me as protective around her. She's in charge, I think. She smiles at me.

'You have Jarrowbrew?' she asks.

'Yes.' I don't add anything more. Neither does Isley.

'Then we can trade,' she says eventually, raising her inflexion on the final word so that it's almost a question.

'Where's the starter motor?' I ask.

'The what?' says the tall man, so I have to turn back to him, and Isley turns too.

'The piece we're looking for.'

'You're a Qitan,' the man says. 'I didn't think they let any in here.'

'I applied for residency under a business permit and the council granted it,' says Isley; mildly, but I can hear his wariness.

'Because of the brew, right? Everyone loves the brew. You brought the good stuff?'

'The best.'

'Let's see it, then.'

Still, neither of us moves. We are in tune. We will not act apart. It's as close as I've ever felt to another being—closer even than during training on the ship over to the war, when the other soldiers were meant to be my family and Coach bound us all together in our heads. We were ready for war. Primed.

'Is that the motor?' I ask, pointing to the rod in his hand.

'No,' says Isley. 'It's not.'

The man raises the rod, swinging his arm freely, exercising his muscles, and then lets it fall back to his side. I tense the muscles of my arms, legs. This place, these faces, feel wrong.

'It's in the cave,' says the woman, 'Do you want to come in and collect it?'

I turn back to her. 'How about we do it out here?'

'Of course. But we must see the Jarrowbrew, okay? Not to hand over yet, if you like, but to see.'

'Okay,' says Isley, like a lamb, and he shrugs off his backpack and lowers it to the ground with care. He unclips the front flap and loosens the drawstring, then reaches in and brings out a small glass bottle filled with the soft pink liquid of pure Jarrowbrew.

'Just one?' she says. The two men flanking her don't speak at all. They're not even looking at us; they both look out over the sea. I keep moving my attention between them all.

'It looks small,' says the tall man. We turn back to him, and it becomes obvious what has the attention of the other men. On the far shore, the coast of Wales, the tall white ports of Swansea are visible, and the first spacecraft of the day are rising from their conical towers. They will depart and arrive every few minutes for the rest of the day—straight up, straight down to the Kissing Gate, which can't be seen by the naked eye. The craft never fly at night. I don't know why; perhaps the locals don't like the disturbance. I remember the cargo shuttles being loud on take-off and landing, at least up close.

'How many does it take?' Isley asks. 'I have three in the bag.' I should have primed him better for this; he'd give them everything. I should have remembered how little he knows of humanity, still.

'Three,' says the tall man, with a nod.

'Then you come in and get the piece,' says the woman, and steps back, into the mouth of the cave. I shake my head, but Isley is putting the bottle on the ground, next to the rucksack, and moving forward without me—he's leaving me behind, we're not acting as one and there's no safety here, we're so far from the inn.

I say, 'No, no, out here,' and the two flanking men turn their attention upon me, frowning at me—no, at something just behind me, and I duck on instinct but it doesn't work and the blow on the back of my head is a vibration, so strong that it drops me down low, to the earth, and my hands take up fistfuls of grass. Another, and another, these blows on my back, spreading out through my arms and only then does the pain start. I hear sounds around me, movements, Isley calls out but I'm apart from him and I try to crawl to him but I can't move, and it's only me and the earth under my knees and the grass in my hands as they do whatever they want to him.

It's like being in space, in the small white capsule they put you in to insert Coach, that injection of a wafer of metal behind your ear while you sit in a hard white chair, and there's an awareness of my own body at an awkward angle—or is this like giving birth? The sensations inside, time passing, building, pain, pain growing, then ebbing.

I want to beg: please don't hurt him. Please don't hurt him.

It's over.

They're gone.

I can move.

I straighten and look around me. They're nowhere nearby. The mouth of the cave is dangerously close. It holds fear for me, but nothing emerges from it.

I see Isley.

I can breathe again, I can breathe.

Isley is on his knees at the cliff edge—when did he move there? He faces out to sea as the rockets rise from Swansea. The backpack is missing, of course, and the suit, and the phrase *of course* begins to play over and over in my head. Of course this couldn't have gone any other way. It's so stupid to have ever thought otherwise. Of course. We were on a path to this. But at least we didn't go in the cave, and down to the beach. We'd be dead now if we'd gone, I'm sure of it, just like in the book. Isley reaching up as they cut him, took tools to him. Of course this was going to go badly, but it could have been worse. I hate myself for that thought, but there it is. It could have been worse. Of course, worse.

'Shut up,' I say, 'Shut up,' and I stand, and go to him. I put my hand on his back and he flinches, and says, 'Oh, no...' drawing it out, until the wind snatches it away from him.

'They're gone,' I say.

'Yes.' He stands, faces me, and I dare to look at him. At first, I see just the blood. Qitan blood is white, creamy, foamy. It's in his curly hair and all over his nose and cheeks, and his wide lips are slick with it. He licks them, but still the blood is there—is it coming out of his mouth? It panics me more than anything that's happened. I fold over the corner of my jacket and dab at his mouth. He says, 'I'm fine, I'm fine,' until I give up. Even now he won't let me touch him.

'Let's go home,' he says.

So we walk home, such a long walk without him to lean on. If only I could let my body sink against his. I'm so tired and sore that I could lie down and die in the grass for wanting to touch him.

I BOLT THE door; this is a private party. He pours the good stuff into two small glasses even though it's not yet midday. I take my usual seat by the bar, the one with the cracked leather top, and he stands, and we drink the first two down. He pours two more.

At least the blood has stopped frothing on his lips. His face, though. His face. The left side of his forehead bulges and his chin has a dent, around which the skin is puffing, darkening.

They didn't hit my face at all. Three whacks was all it took, to the crown of my head, on my back, on my back once more. The bare minimum to keep me down. But Isley's face received their full attention. They wanted to change it, leave their marks upon it.

Of course. Of course.

'I should have known,' I say, and drain my glass again. Isley nods, and follows suit. He pours more.

'Slow down now,' he says, so I sip, and in between the small mouthfuls I find myself saying, 'We'll live. We'll be fine. People. It's people being people. But I should have known. We can't keep the doors locked for too long. It'll look suspicious. We'll work out what to do later. You keep to the kitchen for a few days, and I'll do front of house. I look fine, don't I? They didn't touch my face.'

'You look fine,' he agrees.

'If anyone sees your face, then tell them it's some Qitan thing. Not a virus, nothing like that. A natural thing that happens.'

He laughs, then groans.

'I'm sorry,' I say.

'I'm sorry too,' he says, but still we are not together and I'm desperate to feel it, to feel we belong here, with each other.

But here, on cue, comes the miracle of the brew, bringing the past to the present, telescoping time, and he asks me, 'Tell me where we were when we first met.'

And I say, smooth and soft in the perfect recollection of that moment:

You are steeped in humanity; you have studied their languages and their histories at a speed that puts your invaders to shame and you have come to respect that which you should hate, if you were human. You are young, and curious, and you want to see what it means to conquer, so you travel to Tung Base and offer your services as a translator: Standard Mandarin to Qitan, of course, but also Russian, Spanish, and English.

English is the interesting choice—the language that gets your application noticed. It's a difficult and increasingly obscure tongue, but there are a few Confederate and English servicemen working on the base as part of the Coalition, and their understanding of Mandarin is only just passable, so you will make a useful addition. You walk past the quiet crowds of your people, who have assembled outside the main gates—some to talk, some trade, some simply to look—and enter the seat of power for the first time.

You wait to see the colonel for an age, but eventually you are shown into an office and a small woman greets you politely by touching her own hands together, her fingers curved to lock in position, Qitan-style. She tells you that you will be of great service in securing peace and fostering understanding. Then she gives you complex directions to a food hall; she says it is nearly lunchtime and your unit commander will be along shortly. You take in very little of her speech. You are entranced by the tiny mouth from which her words emerge, words that you have only practised upon yourself.

You have been given an identification card and bracelet,

and you make sure they are both on clear display as you traverse many corridors. You see other Qitans and you greet them traditionally, but they bow their heads and do not look directly at your hands, so you do not ask them for help. This, you think; this is real communication. The unspoken language, a contraction of intention to a movement of fingers and eyes. You know that these Qitans are embarrassed by you, at themselves, and at the parts of themselves that they have compromised. Also unspeakable and clearly communicable. Already you are learning more than you thought possible, but you are a scholar, an adventurer, a traveller: you are different from others. You hold that thought close.

And where am I?

I'm already at the food hall, eating shredded pork with garlic sauce.

I'm not waiting for you. I'm not your superior, or your contact in this place. I have no idea that you are coming. I'm a messenger, one of the few English outcasts given the strange job of reaching the farthest places and leaving printed material for the locals to find, and I've just returned from a long trip to the Nanbu Queeling, where I walked and walked and saw nobody and nothing but gentle slopes and thick rocks turning to mountains. I am very tired and sitting alone at one table in a line when you enter, and look around, and look so obviously lost.

We make eye contact, briefly, and you walk to me and ask my name, in Mandarin. I don't want to give it to you.

'Who are you looking for?' I say, in Mandarin. Coach gives me information about you, your new employment status.

You give me the name. I know it, just enough to be able to tell you that they are not here yet but it's nearly lunchtime and they won't miss that. I promise to point them out when they arrive.

Then you say, in English, 'May I sit and wait, then?'

How do you know I'm English? Is it so obvious?

Later, on Earth, in a bar in Swansea not long after landing you tell me that you don't know how it came to you to speak English. Perhaps it was a premonition of the future. We felt a mutual excitement at the idea. Perhaps language is like that excitement: passing back and forth, awake and crackling, containing the potential for change within it.

But in the food hall we sit, now, with so much ahead and so little known.

We chat. I tell you about my job, and you say that's the reason you became interested in humanity. You read a leaflet—one of the first drops, before the Coalition landed in person. It had turned up, this leaflet, in an area demarcated for refuse—reading material to keep a Qitan busy during bodily expulsion? It amused you, and you ascribed a peculiarly human sense of humour to it that was intriguing, so you took it home and translated it and realised it was a message of peace. That was when you decided to get to know the new arrivals to your planet.

I put so many leaflets in their places. It's a potent connection between us. I leave them everywhere I walk, and I have no idea of the meaning of the land I walk upon. This idea has begun to obsess me.

You represent all that I don't know. More so than the other Qitans on the base, who do not speak my language, because it seems to me that you could communicate it to me, explain your world in a way that I might understand. I want you to find me as interesting as I find you.

I ask your goal in working here and you talk of the desire to see an alternative. Another way of living, and perhaps even another planet, one day. You speak of difference, and of what that might teach you. Of how you have always wanted to feel separate from the world you grew up in.

Separate. That's the word you use. That's the reason why I tell you about the Western Protectorate, a small area of a small country that decided to secede from modern life, from space flight, from the Coalition and the conquering spirit of the new age. I thought I hated my homeland, but as I talk it occurs to me that I miss it.

I tell you that I left it behind because I did not want to be separate any more.

Are you part of this base? you ask.

I tell you I'm not.

I thought not. You sit alone, you say, and if this were a romantic moment I would have said: *I'm not sitting alone now.* I am heavy with programmed responses from the endless old films I've begun to watch through Coach, keeping boredom at bay. I imagine saying those words to you, even that early on in our relationship. I think of it often, and still do, and I think of this conversation when I'm alone, when we're separate, and how I then went on to tell you about my son, existing, growing, living happily without me.

Being so far away feels closer to him, I say, yes, this is what I actually say, and I can't believe I've told you such a thing. I look at you, and you look at me. Then, over your shoulder, I see your contact arriving and I point her out. You say *thank you.* You stand up and go to her. This first meeting is done. I know I'll seek you out again, but I don't have to. Every mealtime, you walk into the room and you look for me. I love the way you look for me.

'Was that how it was?' says Isley.

'I don't know. Was it?'

'I think I almost smelled the pork in garlic sauce.'

'I should have done something today. I should have stopped them. Stopped you from ever going.' It's a deep wound.

'Pain is the greatest of separations,' he says. Then, 'I didn't come up with that. It's part of a saying.'

'I'm sorry.'

'It doesn't matter. It really doesn't matter.'

Someone tries the door.

We don't move. They try again, rattling the handle, and then I hear Dom's voice through the thick wood.

'Jem? You there?'

I go to the door and unbolt it, trying to keep my expression calm, but as soon as Dom lays eyes on me he says, 'What happened?' Then he looks at Isley, and how young my brother suddenly appears as he takes in the damage, like a boy caught up in trouble. I think of Fosse.

'It went wrong,' I tell him, and then I tell him the whole story, only leaving out the guilt that won't ever leave me, for so many reasons, and now for this.

PART THREE

THE STONES OVER the stream, the mossy ground, the leaves of the glade: they have not been welcoming to him. The wind menaced the grasses in the long fields, and the countryside possessed a spirit of its own, unsharing, everywhere and nowhere, like eyes blinking from the dark places of the woods.

Despite all this, Fosse had known he would return to the farm. There was Geography on the timetable before break, and that sense in the air that he was ready for something, some change, that he wanted to find for himself. He had been told not to return, and yet he needed to understand how the man, the stranger, could have taken that farm away from him so easily.

And he wanted his axe.

He moved slowly from trunk to trunk, feeling the rough knots of the wood under his fingers. From his vantage point he could look down over the buildings, and take note of the changes that had already been made. A thin stream of smoke came from the chimney of the farmhouse. A large flat section of tree trunk had been placed beside the door, and a stack of chopped wood piled against the wall. Had they used his axe for the job? He felt his stomach clench at the thought, but could not see his axe on show.

It took him a while of looking to realise that the door was ajar. He concentrated on the black slit of it, bothered by the way it was neither open nor closed. Perhaps the axe was inside, and all he had to do was walk through and collect it—face whatever lay within. Rage and indecision jumbled, morphed into action, and drove him from his hiding place. He ran fast down the slope that led to the nearest wall of the large barn, then pressed himself against it. When nobody called and nothing reached for him, he seized his luck, and ran onwards, around the side, through the barn's open doorway.

The floor of the barn was covered in machinery parts, arranged in meticulous order. A project. An assemblage. What was being built? Fosse picked his way between them, wishing he had paid more attention in Mechanical Life Skills lessons, but nothing looked familiar to him.

As he approached the tractor, he realised the pieces

on the ground had been taken from its carcass; it was exposed and skeletal in places, revealing wires and holes within. One of the women was facing away from him, bent at the waist to look under the wheel arch. He felt her presence as a shudder, a mistake that ran through his body. All the hard work of sneaking and running undone. He stopped still and willed himself into invisibility, but his breathing could not be controlled. He fought it, wrestling to make it flow smoothly through his throat, but panic had set in and the wheezing started soon after, just like it used to when he had been small and scared all the time, with his mother gone away.

It was not just the land that hated him, then—the air itself had turned against him. It was his enemy: it would not flow. He could hear himself gasping. His vision dimmed.

'Hey, hey, hey,' said the woman. He became aware of her beside him. She lightly touched his upper arm. 'Slow down, slow down. Try this.' A light, stiff material covered his head, creating a tent around him. It smelled of oil. He bent over at the waist and looked at his own big feet, in his muddy school shoes, and the sight and smell softened the air, somehow, so that it was happy to slide in and out of him again.

'Stay under there for a bit,' the woman said. 'That's right. Panic attack, is it?'

'I thought the Protectorate had done away with all that shit,' said a different voice, a woman amused, from the far corner of the barn.

'Well, I'm not surprised he's got himself into a state after what Cee said to him. But you know,' said the first woman, intimately now, her voice sneaking up under the material to find him, 'Cee doesn't mean it, honestly, he's just not had the best run with strangers.'

'With anyone,' said the second woman, 'Strangers or not. Which suggests the problem is at least partly his, doesn't it?'

Her voice was getting closer; Fosse was acutely aware, in a rush, of his own ridiculousness. He saw himself as if from above, up with the spiders on the top beam of the barn, his big feet and long legs sticking out from under the tarpaulin, like a child playing at being a ghost. He snatched it from his head and dropped it to the ground, then tried to smooth down his springy, wilful hair with his hands.

The woman next to him wore an intense expression, focused purely upon him, her eyes narrowed and her nose wrinkled—that took him by surprise. 'All right, love?' she asked, and he nodded, and loved her and hated her at that moment. He looked around for the second woman. She was standing between him and the tractor, smiling.

'What's your name?' she said.

'Fosse.'

'I'm Victoria. She's Annie.' He hadn't been mistaken at that first glimpse of them; they were close, somehow, if not similar in looks. Annie was older, he guessed, fatter around the middle and had lighter hair, cut very short, while Victoria wore hers long and loose. Their hair was sensual to him either way. He had immediate thoughts about them both, even though he did not really think they were attractive, not in the sense of what men were meant to want. Their bodies seemed to blend all parts together, within their long knitted jumpers, but their hair, their hair he wanted to touch.

'Pleased to meet you,' he said, not knowing where the words came from and hating the fact that he had used the phrase at all, and they both laughed.

'Charmed,' said Victoria, and rubbed her hands together. She picked at the skin on her knuckles.

'She's trying to get the tractor working,' said Annie, 'with a bit of dismantling, a bit of rebuilding. She's a whizz with all things mechanical.'

'Years of practice,' said Victoria.

'Are these all from the tractor, then?' he asked, caught up in the idea of the two women at work, breathing life into old machinery.

'That's right,' said Victoria. 'I lay them out so I can see where I am.'

'Where you are,' he repeated. He didn't understand. They were here. They were all here.

'In the rebuild. I've done loads of tractors. This is a classic.'

'I'm glad you came back,' Annie said to him. She bent down and gathered up the tarpaulin, and he saw a pattern of thick white hairs at the crown of her hair, like a star in darkness. 'We thought you might run off and tell people we were here, but nobody turned up, did they? So you didn't.'

'I didn't,' he agreed.

'We reckoned this was probably your place to come, you know, to get away, before we turned up. Where you wanted to be alone. We know what that's like. We're looking for the same thing ourselves, to be honest. A place away from everyone else.' She folded the tarpaulin over her arm. 'But you're welcome here anytime, honest. We can even keep out of your way, if you like.'

'He doesn't want to be left alone,' said a new voice. Fosse looked to the door, and saw the man standing there. He looked away quickly. He couldn't bear to hold the gaze, even for a moment.

'Don't scare him, Cee,' said Annie. 'We like him.'

'Is that so?'

He didn't understand what was happening. There was a tension between the women and the man, and he was not part of it, but it was about him. He felt it strongly.

'I just came by,' he said, too loud.

'I can see that.' The man shifted his weight, then put his hands in the pockets of his loose dungarees. This was not a situation Fosse could translate into his own limited vocabulary of life, but he wanted to find the truth in it.

'They like me,' he said, and he heard Victoria laugh, softly.

'It's good land, this,' said Cee. 'We can make something out of it, I think. I've got experience. Ran a place down south. That's all we're after. What are you after?'

The axe. He wanted to look at it again, but he couldn't risk taking his eyes from the man. It would give far too much away. He guarded his expression carefully, and said, 'I don't know. Nothing.'

Victoria and Annie sighed, as one, in time, and their bodies loosened. Their relaxation brought home to Fosse what the question had really been about. Did he want a woman? Two women? Would he ever admit to that out loud?

'You want to do some work for me now and again, then? I'm setting up the old farm for something. I don't know what yet. Could plant broccoli now for next year, if I can get the seeds. I've got contacts…' His voice petered out. Then he added, 'I can give you something for your trouble, even if it's only a bit of knowledge.'

It opened up an intriguing path—to learn how to be like

Cee, to do the kind of things he did. But the memory of the previous day's meeting came back to him and he said, 'There's some others coming here soon, though. Farmers from abroad. The council agreed to give them the land.'

'Is that so?'

'Shit,' said Victoria, and the mood was soured.

'Do you know when?' Annie asked him.

'I'll find out. I go to the meetings. I take notes.'

'You find out, then, there's a good lad, and report back,' said Cee. 'That'll certainly be worth something special.'

'Like what?'

The man looked around the barn, his eyes falling here and there as if just realising that he had little of value to trade. Fosse wanted to be brave enough to ask for the axe. He willed himself to speak.

'Magic,' said Cee.

'Don't,' snapped Annie. She stepped back. Without her presence next to him, Fosse felt vulnerable again. A contract was being made—a pact—and he had a sense of being bound to something he didn't understand. Magic. An offer made to a boy, not an adult.

'Victoria and Annie and I make magic together. You want to see?'

'What kind of magic? Do you mean a card trick, or something?' He tried to sound disdainful.

'I can't explain it, if that's what you mean.'

'Is it like—old coins that you take out from behind my ears?' Mr Satterly had done that once or twice, then showed him how to palm the coin to keep it hidden. He'd practised for a while, but never got good at it.

'You mean a trick? It's not a trick. It's magic. Real, least as far as I can see. I can't explain how we do it.'

There was a clang of metal on metal from the tractor; Victoria was hitting the wheel arch with a hammer, flinging back her arm, her muscles standing out in sharp relief with every blow.

'Don't,' said Annie, again.

'Right, right. Piss off, then,' Cee said to him, and the moment was broken: Fosse was freed. He looked up at the axe. He couldn't help it. Victoria thought he was looking towards her, perhaps, and she smiled and waved in coquettish fashion. He didn't respond, and her smile dropped away.

He'd missed his chance. Or perhaps not—if he brought back the information, he could still barter for the axe, surely, in the way he'd watched his uncle barter. That dry cool voice. *If you give me this, I'll give you that.*

Annie moved forward to touch his arm again, briefly. 'See you later,' she said. As easily as that, he ceased to exist for all three of them. The tractor became the focus of their attention. Annie picked up the tarpaulin and moved it over to Victoria, and Cee followed along behind.

Fosse tried to maintain a slow, tall walk for a while—just like Cee's—but the urge to run overcame him at the treeline and he sprinted for as long as he could stand, until the sweat prickled on his body, in his hair, and then he walked and strained for breath. His mind felt very clear.

'I NEED TO meet her,' says Dom, after checking our wounds like a doctor and judge rolled into one. In other words, like a big brother.

'There's no need to—'

'She's here, she's not going anywhere quickly, and we need to deal with her.'

'What are you going to do?' I ask him. He stares at me and I roll my eyes. 'Look, I'm sure you have everyone's best intentions at heart but maybe you should just walk away and pretend I never told you.'

'How will that help us?' asks Isley. 'Won will still be here, even if we pretend otherwise, and she can't stay.'

I look at their faces, furious with both of them for being so calm and trying to solve the situation before I've had a chance to nurse my injuries for a while.

'Why do you think we have these rules?' Dom asks, but the question is not directed at Isley. He's asking me.

'Fuck off,' I tell him.

'I need to talk to her. Where is she?'

'She's in the basement,' says Isley. 'This way.' He steps out from behind the bar to lead Dom to the back stairs.

'I'll go down alone.' That's Dom's voice, in the hall. Surely Isley won't agree to that? But there's no response, and then everything is quiet.

I tidy up the glasses from the brew we drank together, only a few minutes before, but life has played its usual trick of changing everything that should be solid so that there's nothing left to be certain of. I can't stand it, not so soon after sharing our first meeting, reliving it in the shadow of that attack at the cave—I should throw the glasses at the door, leave shards between us and the world for the feet of whoever comes next. I can picture myself doing it so clearly, right down to the pain in my head spiking with the sudden movement. Is the brew to blame for this vision? It's a hallucination, as if time has split and shown a different possibility, personality. But I blink, blink again, and the vision clears. I haven't thrown the glasses. I wash them, dry them, and return them to the low shelf under the old cash register. It's dusty down there. I'll have to clean it out.

I walk around the room, straightening beer mats, tucking in chairs. I don't touch the full ashtrays from the night before. I find the stale smell of them comforting. I'll do it later.

Something moves fast on my left, coming towards me at speed, and I duck automatically. It's like earlier, at the cliffs, the way my body responds: keep down, keep low. But it's only a bird landing on the windowsill, that's all. A crow. It taps its beak on the glass. It's not looking at me. It fluffs out its feathers, then taps again.

I move slowly so as not to disturb it, treading softly to the hall. Isley is waiting at the top of the stairs, his body tensed, attuned to the conversation happening beneath. He can't hear it, though, surely? How good is Qitan hearing? I can't believe the question has never occurred to me before. Could he have been listening to my breathing in bed every night, from his own room?

I join him and we stand very close together. He doesn't move.

No, I can't hear anything. The low murmur of Dom's voice does not coalesce into the clarity of words, and I'm very tired now, and the brew is leaving me.

'Was it a coincidence?' I whisper. 'You coming to my table? And returning there, so many times? How did we end up here?'

'You told me about the Protectorate.' Isley exhales,

and I feel the soft, warm air on my cheek, my neck. 'You told me about the way you lived, and you sold it to me. You always could sell a story.'

'That's the brew talking.'

'That's not what it does, Jem,' he says. 'I can't do it. I need you to do it.'

'To do what?'

'Make places be better than they are.'

Better, he says. Not real. I'm not capturing real things for him. 'I bought the Lamb and Flag with my tour completion bonus. I asked you to come with me, and make it work. We renamed it the Skyward Inn. You agreed to the name, to the place.' I wet my lips, and say what I've dreamed of saying. 'You wanted me.'

'I still do,' he says, 'but not to be part of me. Can you understand? Not to become part of me. I need you to stay you. Unchanged.' He squeezes past me, and returns to the bar.

I stand and listen to Dom's unclear murmurings. It's all his voice. I can't hear Won speaking at all.

I'm on the point of tiptoeing down a few steps when Dom's voice ends its drone and I hear him coming back up; he catches me there, and raises his eyebrows—that familiar expression, meaning—*I've caught you doing something you shouldn't.*

'Finished?' I ask him.

'You stink of that stuff,' he says. 'Stop drinking so much.'

'It's been a long day. And it's not even noon.'

'That's your excuse? If you start to see double, or feel sick, you'll need to call Doctor Clarke.'

'What did you say to her?'

He looks around the dim hall, with its wood panelling and dusty carpet. 'I told her we'd help her.'

'And what did she say?'

'It doesn't really matter what she says, does it? It doesn't change that our options are pretty limited at this point.'

'Have you got any other contacts?' I ask him. 'Ones that don't prefer stealing to doing a deal?'

His eyes slide away from mine. So he does feel some guilt for what happened. 'I asked around. That's what I got. I don't know these people, Jem. This is not how I do things. You think politics and crime are part of the same thing.'

'It's all getting what you want at a price, isn't it?'

He sighs, and rubs his eyes.

'So how will we get the suit back?' I ask. 'And the part we need?'

'I don't know. Stop drinking so much. I can't bring Fosse here knowing you're like this, with everything that's going on.'

'He's sixteen. You can't *bring* him. If he wants to come, he'll come.'

'Good thing he doesn't want to come, then,' says Dom, and walks away, secure in his victory, in the pain he's caused me. My hatred for him threatens to overwhelm me, but I control my desire to call after him, to try to win an argument that can't be won. I hear him say goodbye to Isley, and the door opening. Voices float in. The regulars are here, and they're complaining about the door being closed to them.

'That's not a welcome,' says a voice, possibly Dave Linkfold who would have just finished delivering the milk, and I somehow manage to put on my professional smile, and head out to show them all what a welcome is while Isley retreats from view.

They come in with suspicious glances around the dirty bar. 'Isley,' calls Dave, 'What's on today for lunch?'

He doesn't answer.

'I'll let you know in a bit,' I tell him. 'You want a drink?'

'Miserable bugger,' he mutters, as he sits in his usual spot. That's all it takes to turn someone against you— one instance of not being the thing they want you to be.

* * *

Minutes of council meeting 25th September

Meeting began.

Mr Samuels is making a bigger request box but can't give an ETA due to being very busy with his own work.

Requests sorted and discussed.

It was agreed to try to update first aid kits and get training. Possible apple trade? Surplus of apples needs to be used before they go bad. Put people on making authentic Protectorate apple sauce? Could the school do that? How long does that last? Reverend Sumner said she had some old recipe books and would look into it.

Reverend Sumner made a joke about holding a mass apple bobbing for Halloween. Doctor Clarke spoke about the dangers of apple bobbing.

Higher Council business: water rates to go up due to drought and maintenance issues.

More quarantined locations (flesh-eating virus?). Doctor Clarke to attend Protectorate meeting about symptoms to look out for, then let villagers know. Possible leaflet campaign. Stocking up on antibiotics.

Tourism plans put on hold due to quarantines.

New family due at Valley Farm by end of October.

AOB. Village meeting called for tomorrow (26th September). To be held at Skyward Inn. Word to be passed round urgently.

End of meeting.

'END OF OCTOBER,' said Fosse.

Annie nodded. She was knitting, in front of the fire. Fosse found sitting with her to be a strong shield from the world and its negotiations, taking away all worry about what he should or shouldn't say.

'What's it going to be?' he asked her.

'A jumper,' she said. She leaned forward and added, conspiratorially, 'For you.'

'Really?' He felt honoured, but also worried about accepting such a gift, and explaining it to his uncle. And the jumpers both Victoria and Annie wore were horrible. Had she knitted those? He wondered if his concerns were written on his face, because she laughed and said, 'It's okay. You don't have to wear it.'

'Okay.'

'Hide it away in a drawer somewhere, if you like. It's a gift, from me to you. No wearing required. Put some more water in my cup, will you?'

He took her cup from the small table beside her, and refilled it from the old kettle hanging over the fire, taking care to cover the handle with a cloth to avoid burning his hand. The domesticity of it had a glamour. It was nothing like at home. Annie's presence made it small, and desirable, and enclosed. With Victoria out in the barn and Cee hunting in the woods, she was the Mistress of the Farmhouse, and she kept it clean and cosy. He had made the title up for her, but it felt like it could be a very old position, going back to an epic age of princes and damsels and monsters to be slain. After an adventure, there must be a place to come back to, and a woman keeping it ready.

'Thanks,' she said, as he replaced the kettle. 'You'll make someone a great husband one day.'

'I'm not...' Fosse said. Not what? He couldn't find a way to finish the sentence.

'My mother taught me to knit,' she told him. The needles clicked until the row was complete, and then she turned the material over and started again. 'And to do all sorts of things. Useful things. She was a computer programmer in Truro when the separation went ahead, and she had to teach herself a whole new set of skills. She got books from the library and learned preserving, self-sufficiency. Even a bit of bee-keeping. Then she had me, and taught me. Now I'm teaching Victoria, but she doesn't really want to learn. She's all about the mechanical things, that one.'

'Is she your sister?'

'What made you think that? No, I met her a few years ago at a party. Do you go to parties?'

Fosse shook his head. 'Some of the boys have parties, though,' he added.

They weren't really parties. The boys met up behind St Luke's and drank brew. At least, they claimed it was brew. Fosse had no idea how they found it. He knew his mother wouldn't sell it to them, so he suspected they were lying about it, as they lied about a lot of things. He had yet to be invited to one of their meetups.

'Not for you, eh? We're all different,' she said. The row finished, she swapped the knitting over and started again. 'I've always loved a party. I met Cee at a party, too, but that was a bigger one. An official one. He wasn't there as a candidate, but just to serve drinks. He took any job he could get, back then. He'd learned to fend for himself, the hard way.'

Fosse didn't know what a candidate was. 'Official?'

'Council arranged,' she said, shortly. 'I never did care for being told what to do. Cee and Vick and I have that in common. All we've found between there and here are people who want to tell us what to do. You'd hate that too, wouldn't you? You wouldn't believe the things that have happened. People can be so...'

'Yeah,' said Fosse.

'All we wanted was a place of our own, and then they started saying we couldn't leave. Not even free to *leave*. They made my mother stay put, too. She's still there. But it's too late to go back now and get her.'

He couldn't follow it, had no idea what she was talking about. Did it matter? She was confiding in him. This was her past, her beginnings. And he knew something about being told what to do. He'd overheard his uncle muttering to himself in his study, preparing for the big meeting at the Skyward that was going on right now. *Have to make them...* his uncle had said. *Have to get them to...* Fosse had gathered up his notebook and pen, waited in the hall to leave for the inn, only to be told by his uncle that he was not allowed to attend.

Trust me when I say you want to keep out of this, his uncle had said from the landing, looking down over the banister.

It never was about choice, after all.

He wanted to ask about the magic, and what Cee had meant by it, but Annie kept on talking, about her mother and her hands, and about escaping nets, slipping away—making little sense. He listened, and drank her in. The world was against them both, but it was outside, and when she finally remembered that he was there, and asked him, 'What about you?' he found he had plenty to say about his mother and his uncle, and the things he wanted to escape from too.

'OKAY, HERE'S THE thing,' says Dom to the packed room, over the heads of the council members and the regulars and the townspeople who never usually come to the Skyward. 'We have a situation that I think we, as a community, need to make a decision about. It's an important decision. It'll reflect on the kind of people that we are, that we want to be.'

He's playing the morality card early. It repels me, that level of obvious manipulation, but that might well only be because I know him and his oratory tricks so well. He used to make speeches to our parents on the reasons for declaring independence, and even went to the British Parliament before the separation to make the local case. He wore a blue suit and a white bow tie, and I remember his nerves—he said to my parents, *I can't do it, I can't do it,* and they pushed him forward and then it was done.

Sincerity takes practice; he must have been working hard on this speech, and on this terrible idea of his. But with no better thoughts between us, there was nothing to do but agree to it. 'We all know Isley,' he says, and points across the room to the bar, where Isley stands beside me, his bruises and lumps nearly faded, his smile nervous. 'He'd give anyone the help they need, and he's never turned away a customer, even when all they had to trade was a mouldy potato or two.' This elicits a warm ripple of appreciation. Blight hit the potato crop badly again this year, but the pink firs continue to stand up well against it. People who planted Maris Pipers, dreaming of creamy mash, are idiots.

A few of these idiots are here today, mixed in with the hardened, pragmatic faces I know better. It's been a long time since a call has gone out for a general meeting. The curiosity of the room is ravenous. It's scaring me, but I keep smiling too, just like Isley, as Dom pushes on with listing all the benefits of having Isley here.

'And we all know about his great brew,' Dom says, 'Right? The best thing to come out of Qita. He's become local to us. We're a welcoming community—and Isley's acceptance proves that.'

A few people shift in their seats. Can't he see he's

laying it on too thick? He reads the room, and changes tack. 'But enough of how great we all are, right? I'll put away my pompoms. We're not American, after all, are we?'

That's all it takes to reclaim them. Everybody still loves a joke about Americans, even though we're all meant to have no idea about what's happening over there and it's entirely possible that way of life imploded too. Perhaps that's the reason we still have a collective idea of who they are—to shape who *we* are. The excess, the disposability, the opulence of their air conditioning running from coal while the world burned, has become legendary. America's a brave blind hero with a fatal flaw, in an old story that we still like to tell.

I see what Isley means about how a story makes things better. Not real, just better.

'So let's deal with this straight. Isley's not one of us. He has a place that he came from, a place in the stars. And although he'd be the first to say that he loves it here, he does still have commitments and friends back home. You don't stop caring about a place just because you move away, do you? My family has direct experience of that.' He looks meaningfully at me, and people turn, and nod. I'm to play my part in all this. 'My sister has been working here for years now, after returning from her travels and bringing Isley back with her. Because she knew he'd fit right in, and he'd help her to make this place work.'

My face hurts from smiling. I wish I didn't hate him so much at times, but it's an old hate that's like a long-healed injury; it only flares up every once in a while, and it'll settle back down to bearable levels.

'But that doesn't mean he's forgotten or abandoned his own people. So when a family friend turned up unannounced on the doorstep right here, in trouble, he let her in. He knew it was wrong, but sometimes we all make decisions with our hearts rather than with our heads. So he let her in. And she's here now.'

The room murmurs, voices rippling louder as they take it in.

Dom shuts it down quickly. 'So it seems to me that you should all be given the opportunity to have a say in what course we pursue—'

'She's Qitan?' says Benny Sykes.

Dom's hold is broken. Everyone starts to talk at once. He's clever enough to let them go, to stand back as they have their say to their neighbours. An unwanted, uninvited Qitan on their soil. It's an emergency. It deserves loud words. Dom holds his nerve for an admirable amount of time. I feel like a sentry on guard, standing so still behind the boundary of the bar. It's ridiculous, but I feel protective of both of them: Dom and Isley, my responsibilities. This has to go well. It has to.

'It's not a question of whether she should be here or not,' says Andy Pocock. 'She's already here.'

A number of voices agree.

'...against the law,' rides over the top of the crowd. I don't see who said it.

They talk on.

Nobody asks how she got here. I suppose nobody wants to know. They like to imagine the borders are unassailable and she simply appeared through sheer strength of will, so her determination can then be a point either in her favour or against her. She's a hero or a villain, depending on what they decide. But which will it be?

Eventually the energy of the room starts to subside, and Dom holds up a hand. He doesn't try to speak until they're quiet. 'We could turn her over to the authorities,' he says. 'And if that's what we all decide, then that's fine. She accepts that, and Isley does too. Nobody's trying to get away with anything. But if we decide she can stay, just for as long as she needs until she can leave safely and quietly, then we all need to be in agreement, okay, and keep her presence here to ourselves. And I think the best thing I can do now is bring her out so you can meet her. People deserve that, don't they? They deserve the right to meet the people who'll be most affected by the decisions they make.'

Do they? If there's been any statement made today that I'd call ridiculous it's that one. But it passes without comment, and Dom continues, 'Isley, could you go fetch Wanda, please?'

Isley doesn't even pause. He moves from the bar and out to the hall, and with him gone the crowd is louder, more relaxed. It's as if they didn't really feel that they could be themselves with him in the room, even though he's seen many of them at their worst over the years, drunk and mournful, or raging against people on the other side of the border, who give such bad deals because they can. It's always trade, always. What will these people demand in return for leaving Won alone? Dom is hoping that they'll do it to feel better about themselves. I'm not so sure.

Isley returns, with Won—or Wanda, as she's now being called—behind him. I've not seen her in any other position but seated, in the cellar, since that first night. It's a surprise to be reminded that she's bigger than Isley, taller, with broad shoulders. Or perhaps the dress she's wearing—a bad choice—enhances the muscled breadth of her upper body. Who decided to tart her up? How willing was she to go along with this? But she's playing it shy, and standing very close to Isley as they wait in the archway. They're not holding hands, at least. Dom wasn't quite that shameless.

The room falls silent again.

'Hello, Wanda,' says Dom, 'Thanks for coming in.'

'It's no problem,' she says. Her voice is quiet, pleasant, with an accent that could be described as posh. *The Queen's English*, that was the phrase for it. Did she learn the language with Isley? Did they watch old Earth films together, once upon a time? 'Thank you for holding this meeting. I'm so sorry to have put anyone to any trouble.'

'You came to see Isley.'

'Yes. A family matter.' Isley nods. They're so well-rehearsed. I wish I had been made aware of this part of the plan, but it's all new to me. I try to keep my face soft and open, but I feel it hardening, closing against the idea of portraying them as linked so intimately that it would be cruel to separate them. I wrap my arms around my stomach.

'We're working to get you home,' says Dom.

'I'm very grateful. I'm so sorry.' She fingers the buttons on the front of the dress, and I realise that it's one of my own dresses, from before I left home. It must have been mouldering in the back of my old wardrobe for years. It was my favourite dress at the time Fosse's father came to stay, and he was conceived. I never could bear to throw it away.

No wonder she looks squeezed by it. It's not her size at all. But somehow it works in her favour; she looks vulnerable, with her flat chest distorting the buttons, and the printed flowers on the pink material riding up at the waist. The crowd is warming to her. It might be enough.

'Right, then,' says Dom, and Isley leads Won away again.

I have an urge to speak, and I push it very far down inside so that nobody would even suspect that I want her to get out, get out, just get *out*. They could turn savage, act like the people of Simonscombe, and I wouldn't care, just as long as she was gone.

'Shall we take a vote on it?' says Dom.

'HOW CAN WE get the suit back?' says Isley.

'I don't know. I'll keep looking into it. Now we've got everyone on our side, I can ask around more openly. But the risks are always going to be high. For all of us.'

I should be behind the bar. I can hear them all getting rowdy upstairs, and it's only a matter of time before they start calling for service, but I couldn't bear to miss this conversation. Not when they're so close to framing me as an outsider.

'Right,' says Isley. 'Right.'

'I need to get out of this,' says Won, and plucks at the front of the dress.

I can't help myself. I say, 'I'd like that put back in my wardrobe, thanks, Dom.'

He shrugs, and says, 'I didn't think you'd even spot it was one of yours. It's been in that wardrobe for years.'

'It has sentimental value,' I tell him. I hate that phrase. I can't believe I've just used it.

'Thank you for the loan,' says Won. 'So sorry.'

'It's fine,' I say, 'but it's not going to work for long. Votes and dresses. They'll still want you gone.'

'I want to be gone.'

'So let's find the suit and get the part,' I snap, and nobody replies. Isley moves from Won, who sits back on the piled crates in the centre of the basement, in her usual position. He chooses to stand beside me instead, and leans in; for a moment I think he's going to point out that I should be upstairs serving, but instead he touches his shoulder gently to mine, just for a moment.

'Well, at least you can stop hiding down here,' says Dom, with a sigh. 'Move up to one of the rooms, and make yourself comfortable until I can fix this.'

'No,' says Won, and Isley echoes, 'No, no.'

'No?'

'I should be somewhere else,' she says, her eyes wide, appealing to him. 'Not here, please. Not upstairs. Is there a different place I could be? Further away?'

Dom doesn't reply straight away. It's not how he understood the situation, I'm guessing. He thought they wanted to be together. I was beginning to think the same thing myself, until Isley's shoulder touched mine.

'I think it'll look better if you stay here,' he says, eventually. 'We told everyone that you came to see Isley. It'll look strange if you now decide you don't want to be here after all, won't it?'

'You made people think that we are—together,' Isley says. It's not often he searches for a word; I get the feeling he's chosen this one with great care.

'Yes, and remember, we discussed how that will help—'

'Jem!' calls a voice, upstairs, and another voice joins in, then adds, 'Service!'

I have to go. I leave Isley's side, and Dom keeps talking because that's what he's good at. He'll win out in the end, I've no doubt.

She doesn't want to be here.

I think of that as I climb the stairs to serve brews. I'm still thinking as I smile at a conversation about whether Tom Frescombe has got better looking with age.

'Would you do him, Jem?' says his son, Michael. Michael and his partner Klaus have been slowly taking over the running of the Frescombe holdings, including the farm and the recycling centre. He was a few years above me at school and was always talking about leaving the Protectorate and starting afresh, and he actually did it, which was unusual. Sometimes, when he gets very drunk, he talks about his time abroad, working for one of the large banks. But usually he prefers to talk about how beautiful the Protectorate is, and how the businesses he runs now are free from so many regulations and technological nightmares. He and Klaus are happy, I think, although I'm never quite sure about Klaus. He doesn't talk much.

'I think Tom's always been handsome,' I say, 'and I've always had a bit of a thing for comb-overs.' Everyone laughs.

Tom takes out his plastic comb from the top pocket of his old checked shirt and runs it over the arranged strands of his hair. 'One of these days Mike'll get his own comb-over,' he says. 'It's the family inheritance.'

'You are thinning a bit,' I tell Michael. 'Do you mind that, Klaus?'

'I don't mind,' says Klaus. He's never quite lost his clipped accent. He stands slightly behind Michael, not exactly in the main group around the bar.

'See? Comb-overs are sexy,' I tell them all.

'Perhaps I stand a chance with Isley's new lady friend, then,' says Tom, getting the biggest laugh so far, and I keep my grin in place.

'Let poor old Isley have his girlfriend,' says Michael. 'He's been alone too long. Nobody should be so alone.' He angles his body to admit Klaus further into the circle, and puts an arm around his shoulders, but Klaus' expression is not as easy to read. Is he thinking of how he's still alone, in this place, even with love on his side and Tom and the others accepting him, and laughing along? I could understand that. But to talk of such things, to even hint at unhappiness, would be to invite the question: *why don't you just go home, then?*

Dom enters the archway, searches for me, and then pushes his way to the bar.

'Excuse me, lads,' he says to Tom and his crowd.

'You drinking?' asks Michael. 'I'll shout you one, councillor. Business is good so far this year.'

'No, thanks, I just want a quick word with...' I move to the side of the bar and he leans in from his side to say, 'She's staying down there.'

'Right.'

'She's just getting changed, and then you can have your dress back.'

If we were alone, I would tell him that's really not my concern at this moment. I'd say something about plans that I didn't get told about, and how he always takes everything over and pushes me out, to the sides, where I've always been, except in my places, those few places I've found where he didn't want to go. But we're not alone, so I say, 'Right,' again, in a tone that he'll recognise.

He hesitates, then says, 'Keep an eye on them.' And he's off, out of Skyward Inn, and no doubt glad to see the back of it for the time being.

Which is how I like it.

HE WAS LOST in thoughts of magic when he heard a soft knocking at the front door, at the beginning of the evening, and assumed something fantastic had finally come for him.

It was only Mrs Satterly, from the council.

'Is your dad in?' she said, and Fosse felt such confusion; what version of events was this? What did she know that he didn't? Then he realised she meant his uncle, mixing up the relationship because she wasn't thinking clearly: her body was shaking, and her cardigan sleeve was ripped at the cuff. Something was wrong.

He left her on the doorstep and called up the stairs. 'Uncle Dom!'

No reply.

'Uncle Dom!' He didn't know what else to say other than the name, but he kept repeating it with an urgency that he hoped would get through the study door.

'What?'

'Mrs Satterly is here.'

'What?' There was the sound of the door opening, and feet on the landing, and then his uncle appeared, poking his head over the banister. Then he was coming down the stairs, his feet bare and neat on the wood. He pushed past and said, 'Freya,' in a tone that was all surprise and warmth.

'Oh, Dominic,' she said, sounding so overwrought. It was like standing on the side of the stage, having to play a bystander in one of those terrible plays that the girls at school made up during drama lessons. He had never once managed to feel involved in their dramatics.

'Come in, come in,' his uncle said, and Fosse obediently stepped back so they could go into the kitchen. Mrs Satterly sat in the nearest chair to the door and put her elbows on the table, her hands to her hair, shuddering. Fosse manoeuvred past her to the corner, and kept silent in the hope of staying unnoticed, so he could stay.

Mrs Satterly's sleeve looked like it had been pulled until the wool had laddered; the strands hung down, drawing attention to her hand, which was very dirty, with the ends of the fingernails blackened. Ash? Blood? The streaks along the fingers looked like mud to Fosse, he decided, but she was clean apart from that one hand, her skin very pale, and her curled hair neatly in place.

'Where's Bailey?' she said. 'Where's Bailey?'

'Where did you leave him?' said his uncle.

'He ran away,' she said, forlornly.

'Would he have gone home?' He fetched her a glass of water, and placed it in front of her. She ignored it.

'He was with me, but he ran away.' Her face contorted for a moment, but she wasn't quite crying. 'He knows the way from the graveyard.'

'That's where you were?'

'To say goodnight,' she said, with a hint of indignation, as if she hadn't considered anyone would behave differently. 'They never should have given up coffins. All that feeding the soil, not wasting wood business. I like the tree, though. They planted cherry. Bob liked cherries.'

'Was… someone at the graveyard with you?' asked his uncle, sitting in the chair opposite her. The legs scraped along the tiles, and Freya looked up from her sleeve to scan the room.

'Have you redecorated?' she said.

'No, it's the same.'

Fosse couldn't remember ever hearing somebody ask that question before; it was a throwback to a different mindset, he suspected. A polite thing to say back when people changed their rooms all the time.

'Freya? Was there someone there?'

'No, no. But Bob was there.'

'He's buried there,' Dom said. Fosse felt his facial muscles pull into a smile. He carefully relaxed them back into a neutral expression.

'I know that,' she snapped. 'But the ground by the tree, the soil, was different. And he was in there.'

'Different how?'

'Softer,' she said. She hummed, and said something under her breath that Fosse didn't catch, then said, 'It hasn't been raining.'

'No.'

'It was like jelly, and I put my hand in, and Bob held it. Under the soil. He held it.'

'You felt something grab you?'

'Bob did.'

'Okay,' said his uncle, in that patient, unbelieving tone he knew well. It could be used in response to many things—a multipurpose attack on tall stories of all kinds.

'He did!' Mrs Satterly said, indignant.

'How did you know it was him?'

She thought about it, then said, 'Who else would hold my hand?'

'All right,' said his uncle. 'All right.'

'We stayed that way for a little while,' she said. 'It was fine. It was fine. I wasn't scared. But then I realised I couldn't feel my own fingers any more—everything was sort of mixed up under the soil—so I pulled free and then something snagged me. Caught my sleeve. I didn't see what it was, but it wasn't Bob. And then Bailey ran away. Poor Bailey. Poor Bailey.'

Fosse watched her cry. It was not a performance. There was something so real about her face. Whatever she felt, she believed, was written there. This wasn't a drama lesson. He began to feel his way towards the difference between the two—the fantasy of heightened emotions versus the ripped edges of reality—and there was disappointment, and a kernel of care for her that he hadn't even suspected existed inside him. He did love her, in some form, and he didn't want her hurt. It was a revelation. There was goodness inside him.

'I'll go find Bailey,' he volunteered, wanting her to feel better, ashamed of his initial excitement at her pain.

'Would you?' she said, 'Oh, please, I think he'll have gone home.'

'I don't think—' Dom began, and Fosse said, 'I'll be fine,' trying on responsibility, maturity, in his voice.

'Oh, please,' said Mrs Satterly, again.

'Just get the dog and come straight back here, okay?'

'Yeah. No problem.' And part of him was determined to do that. Like a good man, he thought, as he fetched his coat and the big torch, and set out.

*   *   *

BAILEY WAS IN the Satterlys' vegetable garden, sniffing at the sprout trees under net. The dog must have jumped the small fence to get inside. Fosse couldn't see how he'd managed it. He was shaped like a barrel, and it took an age to persuade him to lumber out through the gate. Fosse looped a piece of rope from last summer's bean poles around Bailey's neck and tugged, but he couldn't bring himself to be harsh, and eventually the dog decided to get up and leave of his own accord. Then he seemed happy enough to stroll alongside him, although anything faster than that was obviously not going to happen.

When Fosse took the turn to the church, Bailey didn't complain.

He had never held a dog on the lead before, and he'd never seen Bailey on the receiving end of one either, but the dog ambled by his side as if a mutual agreement had been struck, keeping him amiable company through the almost empty estate, over broken flagstone drives and overgrown hedges in the last light of day, and to the outskirts of the village, and St Luke's.

When they reached the lych gate—an old carved wooden arch—the dog sat down. He didn't seem panicked, but something about the way he settled on his haunches suggested he wasn't thinking about getting up again.

'All right, then,' said Fosse. He tied the makeshift lead to the arch and left the dog there.

The last time he had been in the graveyard was for the lowering of Mr Satterly's body into a large hole. It had been wrapped in one of the special blankets that was meant to encourage organic breakdown—Fosse had no idea how that worked—and then the sapling had been placed and the hole filled in. Where had that taken place? A way back from the entrance, he thought. The oldest graves bore stones still, and the trees began in regular order further back. He moved towards them at speed, not quite running, not quite walking.

He wished Bailey had agreed to come along. The doughy head and fat paws gave reassurance. He wanted his own dog; he hadn't really thought of it before. He wanted an animal to love him and uncomplicate him. It would be easier to be himself in the presence of a dog than with women, or men. Although it occurred to him that he might affect the animal rather than its good nature rubbing off on him. It might be ruined by becoming his property—take on his doubts, his darkness.

No. Better not to have a dog.

Miriam Elizabeth Trench

Many of the gravestones were unreadable, with moss thick in the grooves, blurring out the letters, but some were legible. There were still Trenches in the town. Mrs

Trench was a lacemaker. Anna and Beth Trench were annoying twins, three years below him in school. Their dad, Damon, was a tinker, going from house to house all over the district with a tray that folded out to create a table packed with goods. He liked to present them with a flourish and say: *Take your time, take your time, everything negotiable.*

James Brownlee
In Peaceful Slumber

Brownlee was a common name. Fosse knew quite a few, and this could be a relative of any of them. The dates were obscured by the moss. He wished he could stop reading the stones. He sped up to a jog. Only snatches of names and phrases leapt out at him.

Triffold
Good father
Angels
Langleigh
Staldish
Too soon

Then he was past the stones and into the trees with the carved wooden plaques underneath, too small for him to read, sticking up from the earth. The trees were bare-branched and bereft as the last of the light faded.

Fosse switched on the solar torch and slowed his steps.

He remembered a science lesson about trees—the way the branches above were mirrored in the root structure, easily as big below as they were above. The bodies of the dead were tangled among those roots as the trees grew and fed, ensuring harvests of apples and plums, damsons and walnuts, and cherries. Cherry season started early in June, and two weeks of the school year were given over to what they called Food Technology, which involved drying and jamming and preserving. Design lessons then followed, so they could hand-draw labels reading:

Western Protectorate
Certified Organic
Home Grown, Bee Pollinated
Cherry Jam

The list of ingredients never mentioned the bodies that seeped into the trees, but Fosse supposed that was the way of all dead things, really, so there was no reason to make it plain. The world wanted to function without thinking about it.

Then the lessons in Business Management. They

tracked invoices around the world, and even into space. The Coalition military in particular had a taste for their cherry jam, and it was ferried regularly to the Swansea spaceport to make the journey to Qita. All the graveyards in the Protectorate, all the roots and branches spreading up and down and out, and onwards.

The newly planted trees seemed spindly, vulnerable, and the ground felt a little softer underfoot. The texture reminded him of the muddy field at Valley Farm, and he found he wanted the axe again, strongly. Something to wield. What had Mrs Satterly said? The soil was like jelly. She had put in her hand.

The newest trees were as small and delicate as babies. Fosse found the right place, checked the small plaque by the weak light of the torch:

Robert McKendrick Satterly
A wonderful husband, taken too soon

But he had suffered and suffered, and they had all seen it, and the traders had negotiated at the meetings to get him the painkillers he needed. Surely his death had been a relief to everyone. It certainly had to Fosse, who had hated sitting next to the thinning grey streak of pain who had once been Mr Satterly in council meetings. He had not been quietly fading away but intensifying, getting sharper and sharper in agony to the point where it pierced Fosse simply to look at him.

The words were all wrong. Surely Mr Satterly had not been taken soon enough.

The soil looked clean, undisturbed. Fosse knelt down and put his hand to it.

It was wet. He felt the moisture soak through the material of his trousers in seconds. It would have been easy to push his palm down into the sodden earth. But the roots, the roots and the body and the pain, captured, being sucked up and spread out and taken into the cherries, stopped him. There was fear in the soil. It could so easily slip inside him, travel up his arm, and he would never get rid of it. It would become part of him.

He took his hand away and stood up.

There was nothing here to see. He started to retrace his steps.

The sense of leaving a living presence behind him was so strong that Fosse found himself looking back over his shoulder. There were only the trees. No birds. No bats making circles in the night sky. The branches were black cracks in his vision. He had to fight his impulse not to look back again.

Bailey was by the gate.

The dog got up, stretched out its hind legs, and looked at him expectantly.

Would he admit to going to the graveyard? To touching the wet soil? Fosse knew it would complicate matters. He should not have been there—that would be the starting point, no matter where the conversation ended.

Fosse undid the rope from the arch and began the return journey, looking forward to reuniting dog with owner. He was capable of caring about the dog, and about Mrs Satterly, and about life. Annie was making him a better person.

ISLEY POURS ME another, and I start to talk.

The sight of Zay Shines flows out of me. I have no idea why it's in my mind, but once I start to talk of it, I can't stop, and I don't want to. It's an archipelago—a chain of tiny islands off the coast—and it's holy. Or it's forbidden. It's the scene of some sort of massacre, but I was told no more about it than that in my briefing. It was one of my last missions, and a lot of what happened there I put down to my own tiredness. Reading human traits into Qitan behaviour.

Do you know what happened there? No, I know, you won't speak. It's only that I've always wondered if it was a holy place before the terrible thing happened—whatever it was—or if the event caused the Qitans to enshrine those hundreds of hillocks in the still water. The ocean that nobody sails. Here be monsters? I don't know. Coach would draw a blank if I asked. I was told, sotto voce, after a briefing, that life forms had been detected there and there were suspicions from their movement patterns that they were sentient. Quiet exploration was happening further down, at a deserted stretch of coast, before I left to return to Earth. I wonder what became of that. They thought the Qitans wouldn't know what they were doing.

I've known since Zay Shines that the Qitans always knew exactly what we were doing.

The bright, broken ground leading to the still water.

I'm wearing sunglasses with my uniform, and the tinted lenses turn the sky purple and the ocean red. But the ground is still a shining white, cracked, as if parched. It feels wrong that there's a chill to the breeze. Is the water cool or warm? I'll never know.

If places bear the echoes of the events that happen upon them, then that might explain this profound, pulsing feeling inside me. Is this what the Qitans in attendance feel? They have set up small tents along the shore for miles, and they sit on their knees, just inside the brightly coloured flaps. Each tent bears a swirling pattern on its roof, and has a pole erected opposite it, at the very edge of the shoreline.

The swirls provoke a strong response in me. I don't want to look at them, to feel sucked in by them. I don't want to be here anymore. But I have a job to do. I must leave at least one leaflet, with its message of peace, acceptance, domination. Whatever you call it.

Just do it, and be gone.

Is that *my* voice in my head, or is it Coach?

I approach one of the poles. I have no intention of taking down or even covering what's already there. I can attach it to the midpoint of the pole, so they can rip it down easily enough if they choose to. I don't think they ever do, but they could. Isn't that enough? To leave them with the option?

They don't move as I approach the pole.

I touch it.

It's slippery. Cold.

I look back at the tents. Nobody is looking at me. Not one Qitan has turned their eyes in my direction. My actions do not exist for them. They are erasing them before I even start.

I think of you.

I think of you in the cafeteria, holding my gaze. We've spent every lunchtime together for over a year. I feel the places where our languages don't quite meet, but I believe there's something deeper than surface understanding, and I feel it with you most when you make the effort to pretend for my sake. Our lunches have become the thing I look forward to. You make me feel seen.

Here, I am not seen. The Qitans do not see each other, for that matter. Unlike Langzin Square, there is no trade happening here, no communication. They sit in their tents, marked by their poles, and do not talk. They are not together. There is no shared faith at work in this place. It's not holy at all. The briefings speak of Qitans as a monoculture. Imagine being human and thinking that any intelligent civilisation could be totally in agreement.

Imagine being Qitan and seeing humanity that way. As a hive mind, all sharing the same thought—to swarm over this planet and make it their own. Is that how they see me? As less than an individual?

Is silence their weapon? I don't understand them.

My fingers shake, slip on the pole, and the leaflet flutters away from me. The breeze picks it up and carries it to the shore, and beyond. It lands on the surface of the ocean. It creates no ripples. It is still. A white rectangle, with the inked marks upon it already beginning to blur.

Nobody looks at the leaflet.

I approach it, until I'm standing at the very edge of the water. I hold my breath and lean over, trying to reach it, and the feeling that I'm doing something wrong pulls me back. I can't pick it up, I can't fish it out. It floats away, although there's no current. One corner submerges, and the rest follows its path in slow grace. The water is opaque; the leaflet is lost to view.

I step back, and realise the hillocks have moved.

They have drawn together, away from the leaflet, recoiling from it.

I omit this from my report. At first, I don't understand it enough to shape it. Later, I persuade myself that I misunderstood the place. I put it down to being so drained, so sick of the job. The mind plays tricks. It's strange, the things we choose to speak of, and when we decide to keep silent.

You want me to talk and you give me enough of the good stuff to make that happen, night after night. You feed me more, and more, to the point where I say, I admit to you, that the water was not opaque, and I saw something as I leaned over for the leaflet.

I saw a hand, a human hand. The palm toward me. The fingers splayed.

The hand belonged to my son.

'How could you tell?' says Isley, breaking through my words, bringing me back to the bar.

'I—'

'Are you certain?'

'I don't know.' I try to think back over what I've relived, but the clarity is gone. I've drunk far too much. More than ever before. He kept pouring and pouring, as if he wanted something in exchange for his generosity, and I've given it, but now he's afraid of what it means. *I'm* afraid of what it means. I'm afraid of why Isley is pushing.

'Think back. Think it through.'

'Please don't...' I can't make sense of it.

He shakes his head, but it's not in a human way, not dismissal or irritation. Perhaps it clears the effect of the brew. I try it, and feel a little better.

'Your son's hand,' he says. 'You saw your son's hand.'

'Is that what...?' Yes, that's what I said, and no, that's not true. I never saw his hand, or any hand, at Zay Shines. How would it even have been possible to see an adult hand and know it as Fosse's, when at the time he was a child who I hadn't seen in years? Would I even know my own hand if it had appeared before me? I lift it up to my face and wiggle my fingers.

'Jem,' says Isley. 'Concentrate.'

'I didn't see that. The hand. I don't know why I said that.'

His chin unclenches, a little. 'You've been thinking about your son a lot. He's on your mind. That's why he snuck in. To your memory. That can happen.'

'I didn't see a hand,' I tell Isley.

* * *

I'M IN THE Skyward, sitting on the customer's side of the bar, on the usual cracked leather stool. It's late, or early. It was a long and busy night, with so many jokes to laugh at and questions to deflect. They wanted Won— Wanda—to come out and talk to them. *We're a friendly bunch. She doesn't need to hide away. Isley, bring out your girlfriend!* But Won won't move from the cellar. She is down there now, sitting still, while we get drunk.

'Are you sure?'

'Don't look so worried,' I tell him, and it's good to have the opportunity to chide him for showing an emotion. 'I'm not losing it.'

'No.'

'I'm fine.'

'You are.'

'Stop saying things in that tone or I'll stop believing it!'

'I'm sorry,' he says, and gives the faintest smile, which drops away again as he says, 'I feel like I should check on Won.'

'Won is fine,' I say. 'I took her something to eat earlier. If she wanted to see you, she'd come up.'

'I feel responsible for her, but you have to believe I don't want to see her,' he says, then puts the stopper back in the bottle and slides it under the counter.

'Why not?' He doesn't answer. My mouth is dry from the words I've spilled for him tonight. His silence feels unjust, and is more than I can bear. 'For fuck's sake, tell me something!'

'Spend some time with your son,' he says. He won't look at me. He picks up our glasses, one in each hand, and clinks them together. They make a small, clean sound.

'I'm going to bed,' I tell him.

He nods.

'Fuck you.'

'What?'

'Fuck you.' It doesn't sound like an insult any more.

'I can't,' he whispers. He still won't look at me. I don't understand him anymore; did I ever understand him?

'I'm leaving.' I manage to get off the stool and edge my way to the stairs. Down leads to Won. She could be awake, listening. Up leads to bed.

I choose up.

I don't attempt to undress. I let sleep take me. Fosse's hand comes to me in a dream, but this time it's his infant hand, as it would have been back then, although I never saw it. His chubby fingers open and close, as if he's grasping for something he can't quite reach.

PART FOUR

'PREPARATIONS,' SAID CEE, and brought the axe down again. Fosse watched, sitting on the ground opposite the front door of the farmhouse. It was a cool day, but bright.

The day after retrieving Bailey, while his uncle went to the graveyard to investigate, Fosse had made a journey to the Recycling Centre. He had long enjoyed looking through the pile of items set aside for whoever wished to take them, and this time he made a real find: a pair of iron bars, original use lost. Perhaps they had been part of a machine. He had put them in his backpack and carried them home, the muscles of his back screaming. A month had passed, and he had used the bars every night as the hours of winter darkness drew in. He lifted them over his head and then balanced them on his stomach as he lay on the floor, lifting his legs, holding them a few inches aloft for as long as he could bear.

He felt certain that he needed to make his body worthy of the axe.

When he was strong enough it would be his, and then he could protect the people he loved from whatever was waiting to get them. Tales of young men coming into their power had long fascinated him. There was always a weapon that they strived to deserve.

People were coming for Valley Farm.

Fosse had looked through his uncle's office a few weeks ago and found notes on the arrivals. The Higher Council's typed page listed ages and skill sets for each member of the family, all six of them including the children, and even the youngest of them—eleven years old—had enviable abilities. *Computer skills*, read the document. *A basic understanding of solar engineering. A certificate in sustainable farming techniques awarded by the Pan-Asian Education Board.* What was the Protectorate, in the face of that? Why would they come to a place like this?

At the bottom of the page was one last statement.

Reason for urgent relocation application: Persecution of Christian beliefs.

'They'll get what's coming to them,' said Cee, and the

axe went down. The log cracked, and split in two, falling away from the blade.

Fosse watched as Cee fetched another log and put it in place. When he had tried to write his own list of attributes, he had failed to write a single sentence. Except for the bit at the bottom.

Reason for urgent relocation application: Because I fucking hate this place.

It was not exactly true, but writing it had made him feel better, as if he had let out something that had been squirming around inside him for far too long.

'They've got skills, you say.' Cee was shirtless, sweating. Fosse put his hands in the pockets of his coat—it was the first time he'd needed one in years. He had overheard his uncle telling Doctor Clarke that new Coalition machines were turning the tide of climate change, so the disease spreading in the south probably wasn't anything to do with an influx of foreign invaders: birds, or insects, say.

Victoria and Annie were not there. Cee had told him that the girls had gone gathering—possibly for the last of the blackberries or the first of the chestnuts. Knowing what could be gathered and when—that was a skill, surely? He decided he would write it on his piece of paper later.

Cee's hands held the axe so well, with a casual looseness, with purpose, with a certainty that it was under his command. He took three heavy chops at the log, and it split. He put a new log in its place. 'You want a go?' he asked.

'No,' said Fosse, as a reflex, *no* being the word he found most often in his mouth in Cee's company. It was as if he wanted to negate the man.

'That's right, you already know how to use it, don't you?' said Cee. 'I remember.'

They had been watching him in the muddy field that day after all. He had known it, but had wanted to pretend otherwise to himself.

'You looked good,' said Cee. 'Chopping away. You could have done with some trousers on, though.'

Fosse wished Annie would come back, and they could be alone together again. He had told Annie all kinds of things, and she had responded with secrets of her own. Things she had witnessed, on her travels across the Protectorate. A black cygnet being stalked and caught by a giant stripy cat, like a tiger, and young children being married to old men in mass ceremonies on village greens. Surviving an attack by people she called slavers. Cee had fought them off with his bare hands. Hearing Cee talk by the light of a bonfire, and deciding he was right about it all. What he was right about, she hadn't said.

Cee knows so many things, she had said, after Fosse told her about that night in the graveyard, with Bailey chained up outside, waiting. *Changes are coming. Cee knows how to live with changes. He's going to protect us all.*

'You know,' said Cee. 'I've been thinking about it, and I reckon we might be related. Your family always been from around here?'

Fosse nodded.

'Thought so.' Cee straightened up and stroked the red handle of the axe. 'I grew up around here, and moved down south later on. I know this land really well.'

'Why did you leave?'

'Got a girl in trouble. Yeah, I reckon we're related. Look at your chin. It's just like mine. Uncanny, really.'

There was a calculating edge to the words that did not escape Fosse in the least. This was a game, a manipulation. Cee liked those. When they were all together, he had said how one woman was prettier than the other, or one had nicer hair, while he looked on to see if the words would do damage, his upper lip raised, his front teeth visible. He wore an identical face now. Mainly Victoria and Annie ignored him when he tried such tricks, so Fosse decided to do the same. He looked away to the woods, hoping to see the women approaching.

'I was a handful back then,' said Cee. 'I bet you are now, aren't you? A wild one. My mum sent me here to live with my aunt and uncle once I got into scrapes a few too many times in Bristol. She thought this would be a better life—with no gangs, less crime, all of that. I never knew my dad. That can be tough, growing up that way.'

It was so obvious. Fosse felt it as a crushing weight: the disappointment, the realisation that Annie had told Cee everything. There had been no private pact. Nothing he had told her had been between them alone.

'What are you, about fifteen? Yeah? Yeah. That makes sense, you know? I used to hang around over at the Skyward a lot. The inn on the other side of the town. Does that ring a bell?'

So he had got his facts mixed up, thinking the inn was possibly owned by Fosse's family. Fosse had told Annie that his grandparents were rich, and his mother lived at Skyward. She must have confused it in the telling. His disappointment hardened, began to turn into contempt.

'No,' he said. Now he knew why the word was always coming to him in Cee's presence. It was the easiest line of defence. Deny everything. 'Never heard of it.'

Cee frowned.

'Haven't you got enough wood chopped by now?' Fosse asked him. He had the measure of the man now. It was all a con. There was no magic, either. He was nearly certain of it.

'I'll need your help with the next bit. We have to sharpen the tops, then put them in pits hidden around the fields.

Whoever turns up to take this place away from us has a surprise coming, huh?'

Pits with sharpened stakes.

'If I had a son,' said Cee, 'I'd like him to be just like you. The girls think so too. That they'd want someone like you to be part of this family. Someone useful. Someone loyal.' He positioned a fresh log and smacked the axe down.

Fosse told himself that he'd take no part in actually building the traps. Let Cee do whatever he had to do; he couldn't stop him, anyway; he was a boy and Cee was a man. It was a comforting distinction to make.

But what if Cee built the traps and didn't reveal their locations? Fosse imagined returning to the farm, running through the woods and fields, and falling into one, feeling the ground give way beneath his feet and screaming, maybe, a scream cut short as the spikes impaled him, ripped through him, and he would bleed and bleed in the pit for hours, for days. Death would take an age to come unless a spike got him through the neck. And Cee would come across his body and would fill in the pit, whistling as he worked. Fosse would become the hand under the surface—the hand he had been dreaming of since that night at the graveyard.

'What's this? Men at work! My favourite thing.' It was Annie: soft, content, deceitful Annie. He was pleased to see her, like a child. Yes, he was young and useless. He knew it.

Victoria followed after, coming around the corner of the farmhouse, swinging a wicker basket. She had twigs in her wild hair. 'I climbed a tree,' she said. 'Great view, right to the sea.' She looked at the hefty pile of logs and said nothing, her eyes sliding away from it. 'Anyone hungry? Or should you be getting back to school before you're missed?'

'Yeah, I should—'

'Who are you to tell him when to stay and when to go?' said Cee, easily. He put down the axe and wiped his hands on his torso, then reached for his shirt, on a peg by the door.

'I should go, though,' said Fosse.

'I thought you wanted to see a magic trick.'

'Magic's not real, though, is it?'

'That's news to me. Come on, girls, let's show him.'

'Not right now,' said Annie, folding her arms over her stomach. 'All right?'

'I told him we were related,' said Cee.

'Is that so? Maybe you are. Maybe everyone's related, in one way or another.'

'Maybe so,' said Victoria, and took a step towards the door of the farmhouse. Cee blocked her path. 'I need to put this basket down.'

'Put it on the ground, then.'

She sighed, and put it down carelessly, but under her irritation Fosse thought he saw something else. She was afraid of what might happen.

'Enough,' said Annie, and Cee gave her a look that shut her up. The power of the look stunned Fosse. She couldn't be blamed for what she told the man, when he could give looks like that.

'Come here,' Cee said, and Annie did as she was told. She held out her right hand and Victoria did the same, palms up. Cee put his own right hand on top, his palm facing upwards too, and said, 'Watch this.'

The three of them created a tight circle, their shoulder hunched, their eyes on their joined hands.

'Any second now,' said Cee.

'It's not working,' said Victoria.

'Sssh.'

'It's going,' said Annie. 'I can feel it. There.' But there was nothing to see. Wait—their hands were sinking, Cee's hand melding into Annie's, into Victoria's, and their skin was no barrier as Cee pushed down. Their fingers merged and pushed out at odd angles. A shared ball of flesh was being created at the end of their arms. Annie let out a low hum, but none of them seemed surprised or bothered by the act. How often had they done this? There was no trick to it, surely. It was real.

'Touch it,' said Cee.

Fosse shook his head.

'Where you going?'

He hadn't even realised he was moving backwards, putting distance between them.

'See? Magic,' said Cee, raising his voice, then, 'Say hi to your mother for me.' He started to laugh, and the sound of his mirth followed Fosse as he turned and ran. Not for school, not for home. For Skyward Inn.

A MONTH.

A month without a drink. I've had no long, slow fall into the past with Isley. I miss it, and I miss him. He spends more and more time in the cellar with Won, even though he claimed that was the last thing he wanted.

Being without him makes me feel clean, emptied of emotion. It's good to know for certain that I'm not addicted to Jarrowbrew, or to him. Not physically.

'I suppose you were always going to ask that question,' I say.

Fosse nods. He worried me when he turned up at the inn, his face strained, asking to talk to me—the boy who never talks. Something in me knew it was about the past, perhaps because we've got no element of the present or the future in common. He sits next to me on the bench, his expression tightly packed with a need that I don't think is in his power to articulate. He's still too young. But he's obviously not a child any more. He can't hide the span of his shoulders by hunching, and there's a shadow of stubble on his cheeks.

'Maybe it was a bit stupid, coming all the way out here,' I say. 'We should have gone back to your uncle's house.' I look out over the Black Torr Hole. It's a small lake—little more than a pond, really—sunken into the dip between hills on the moorland. All I thought was that I didn't want him in the inn, and I steered him out and started to walk. This is where we ended up.

'It's good here,' Fosse says.

This bench has been here for decades. Dom and I used to come here as children, armed with buckets and nets, and when we got bored of catching sticklebacks or scooping up frogspawn we'd sit on the bench, our legs swinging, and argue about something. I remember falling out about all sorts of things, from whether a certain plant was poisonous to whether Qitans really did eat their children. I was so certain they did. Lots of kids at school believed it, but Dom was always against it. I wanted Qitans to be frightening and exotic. He wanted them to be just like us, so there would be no need for any of us to ever leave the Protectorate. If every place is just the same, then what's the point of going there?

Do I start that far back, in childhood squabbles designed to make the world seem a certain way?

'He was never going to stay,' I say. 'He wasn't from here and he had his own life, on the other side of the barrier, and that's the reason why—'

And I talk, talk in pieces, talk in chunks of information, and the act of talking makes talking easier. I talk without the benefit of Brew. I talk without order, without design. I create pieces that Fosse must puzzle over himself, later, alone, pieces like:

- He was here for three months
- We were not in love
- Not as I understand love to be now, which is not saying much
- But you don't need to know that
- It was an exchange, my brother for a stranger
- Both of them interested in politics, in learning about the world
- While I only wanted to speak different languages, that's all I worked towards, back then
- Thinking if there were other languages, there would be a way to say other things
- Reasons, I have to avoid giving reasons
- Dom and Jackson, children, trading places, organised privately by my parents through

government contacts, and Jackson came to us, stayed in our house to learn about the Protectorate way of life, and my parents hated him, and he hated them

- I sneaked downstairs, late at night, wanting milk, something fresh, something cold
- I heard them talking about the way he took everything for granted, and that was the moment that it crystallized for me that I liked him, just for that, just for being able to not be grateful for being alive
- They were in the living room, and the door was ajar; I peeked in
- They had a fire going, and a bottle of their own gooseberry wine, and my mother said—*I wonder if Dom's learning anything apart from how to be spoiled*
- And my father said—*he has to see the other side to understand why this is so important, he won't change*
- I drank my milk and went back upstairs, and he was standing by the bedroom door
- Dom's bedroom door, but his for those months
- He pointed his finger at me and beckoned me in, and he closed the door behind us and said very quietly—*I'm so hungry, all the time*

- I said—*I just drank some milk, it helps*
- I was wondering if he had heard my parents, and I think he had, I'm pretty sure he had, and that's part of the reason why he kissed me
- But I also think he just liked me, and I liked him, and that's okay
- I had other reasons too
- I wanted to know how to get out
- Get out of my life, but I thought getting out of this place, this system, this protected area, whatever you want to call it, would be a start
- But I never thought he would take me away with him, never that
- It was only to be close to someone who didn't know he had already escaped
- At least, that's what I thought, before I realised Dom is right, and we are all the same, in some ways, in the worst ways
- But you don't need to know that
- He was wearing pyjama bottoms and I was in a vest and shorts, elasticated, they stretched, all the clothes allowed and accommodated our hands so easily
- I want you to know that sex is a force for good, and I'm certain your uncle hasn't explained this to you because he doesn't

believe it, or perhaps he just doesn't care
about it

- But I think you should understand that it had
a sense of rightness that comes when nothing
is being forced, or taken, although maybe that
shouldn't be the way to judge it
- Because the ease of it meant I didn't really
think about it, and I don't think he did
either, but I do maintain it was special, it was
meaningful, and not just because it created you
- Although it did create you
- I didn't know that at the time; I didn't know
that until he had left, and your uncle had come
back and—
- His name was Jackson, did I say that? Jackson
Burnham-Carter
- I should have said that earlier
- Your uncle came back and he looked
different, more confident, and he said—*did
you prefer living with Jackson to me, then?*
and my parents laughed and laughed and I
realised, I don't know why, it was something
in the way they laughed that brought me back
to dates and months and how the time was
passing

- Your grandparents wanted me to see someone, get it—get *you*—taken care of, but the guy took the money and never turned up
- I don't remember telling them, I honestly don't, but I remember Dom saying, later, standing in his room—*what the hell were you thinking?* like he was a man and I was a child
- Anyway, you want to know what happened next
- Your grandparents moved away
- No, that came later
- Dom came back and Jackson left
- That's right, and an agreement was reached with his family: money, trade, I don't know much about it, but it was agreed you'd stay here
- They gave you an expensive watch, some sort of remembrance, insurance policy, I don't really understand it, but there was definitely money as well
- I think some of the money was meant for you, you get it later, when you're older, I'll ask your grandparents
- But the agreement was not to contact them unless they instigated contact, so the idea was not to tell you much at all; they thought it would be easier

- So it seems rightness and easiness do not always go together
- And I said that if you asked me I would tell you anyway, no matter what the deal was, and you did ask me, but you were so little, too little, barely talking, or perhaps you were just making sounds and I thought you meant
- *Where's Daddy?*
- I said—*no Daddy*
- I remember that very clearly, and then I realised, that night, in the hours between dusk and dawn
- I should say, I couldn't sleep, not then, not now; I've always struggled to sleep, and that's not because of you
- I realised that night I'd given you no father and a bad mother in two words, that's all it took
- And I thought of Qita, and the story of the monsters who eat their children, and I stole some jewellery from your grandmother and went to Wrecker's Cave, where the smugglers still cross
- I traded for passage to Swansea, thinking only of Qita
- Because it felt like I might belong there But I couldn't find a job on a ship to take me through the Kissing Gate; I was young, I had

no ID, only a sketchy memory of what life was like without Protectorate rules
- The office was at the port
- The Coalition office, and I looked at it every day for weeks—free passage to Qita for a ten-year contract—and one day I went in
- Because if I couldn't belong there, I wanted to break it
- But that's a different story
- Unless you want to know it
- Another time, maybe
- Your dad, is that the word you want to use? your dad, I don't know, I don't know where he is, I never looked for him, I think your grandparents were worried I'd gone looking for him; they never suspected Qita
- Some things are too wonderful to revisit; we have to go to other places, new places, instead
- No
- No
- I'm not sure I believe that. I don't know why I said that
- I feel like I should say something meaningful
- But I'm out of words, and I don't know what else you need to know.

'He's not here,' says Fosse.

'No, he's not here. He was never local. Didn't they tell you that much? Your grandparents. I thought they'd tell you that much.' I find I can't blame my parents, not with any degree of honesty. It was my responsibility to begin with. Fosse remains my responsibility.

'They said he was gone.'

'What about your uncle? Did you ask him?'

Fosse squints up at the weak sun, then says, 'I asked him if he knew my dad, and he said no.'

'That's true.' It's a politician's kind of truth. They were never in the house at the same time, and they never talked. Still, it feels like he's applied a narrow definition to the answer to help himself. Did I do better, though? I failed in every way possible. I will assign no blame, and I will be humble and grateful that I got to have this conversation.

'Your uncle sent me so many updates about you while I was serving,' I tell him. 'I came back hoping we could find a way to be friends. But time passed, and...' And what? I've talked far too much.

He looks at the water. Perhaps he's wondering how quickly he can get away now he has his answers.

'There's people living out at Valley Farm,' he says.

'The new family are here already?'

'No, not—they shouldn't be here. Nobody knows

they're here. But me.' He twists his fingers in his lap.
'They're not...'

'Where are they from?'

'Further south, she said.'

'Who said?'

'The woman. One of the women. The man is making
traps. I saw him.'

'He's a trapper?' It's a profession that's been making a
comeback. Rabbits have become particularly popular in
the markets.

Fosse shakes his head.

'What, then?'

'I dunno.'

What is it he wants to say? Part of me wants to shake
it out of him. 'Tell me.'

'They did something with their hands.'

'What thing?'

'A thing.'

That's when I realise we won't ever be friends. Even
after abdicating my role for so many years, the sheer
amount of frustration he can imbue in me proves that
I'm still his mother. He has to tell me what's wrong, tell
me everything, and every question I ask him bears the
hallmark of an anxious parent. In that moment I recall
it—revealing my pregnancy to them. *What's wrong?*
Over and over. *You know you can tell us anything.*

But he is telling me, as best he can. I'm just not able to understand it. Too much time has passed. Too little between us. I think of the men at the Skyward, and how I get them to talk when they don't even know that's what they need to do. To make sense of themselves.

'Something with their hands,' I say. 'That's weird. What was it like? Like something you've seen before?' I use my light, interested tone. I don't look at him directly, but focus on the sun on the surface of the water, glints of light, broken and scattered.

'Mrs Satterly said the same thing about the graveyard, and the man said it was a magic trick.'

'How many people are there? In the valley?'

'There's the man and two ladies down there with him too, but they're alright.'

'You think they're okay down there, with him?'

'I dunno.'

'Are you a bit worried about them? I'd be worried about them if they're nice but he's not.'

'Yeah.'

The more I find out the worse it gets.

I'll ask around at the Skyward. Nothing happens here without somebody knowing about it, surely.

'He said he might be my dad,' says Fosse.

I'm getting the measure of this man. He's dangerous. A confidence act, trying to win over my son. For what purpose? I've not felt fear like it, sudden and cold, for years—since first leaving for Swansea, or taking off for Qita the very first time. But with it, anger—anger that could shake me apart. I have to struggle to keep my voice calm as I say, 'Do me a favour, okay? Go home, and tell your uncle about it. Tell him to come over to the inn this afternoon and I'll ask around and we'll get to the bottom of it. You don't have to even be involved. All right?'

Fosse nods, and I believe he's relieved. I can deal with this for him. I am his mother, after all, and this is so much more important than Isley. This is real contact. This is a fight.

VALLEY FARM SHOULD have been watched. It was a temptation, a vulnerable spot, just waiting for people to turn up and take it. We let our guard down. We thought the Protectorate was safe.

I look down at the farmhouse, the smoke rising from the chimney, and I think of Won sitting in the cellar. She has claimed that space as hers. I'll never stand in it again without thinking of her. It's shocking, how easy it is to take a place and make it your own.

I'm too angry and scared to think straight. We have to go down to the farmhouse, and I don't know what comes next. I know it involves stepping up to the task of being a mother, and a better person. I need to face these people down for the sake of my son. And I won't get caught out again, not like I did at Wrecker's Cave. This time I'll see it coming.

We start down the hill, through the woods, to reach the farmhouse. The smoke means someone is there. It means something has to be done.

Dom's at the front, leading the way, with Damon Trench beside him—Damon the tinker, who travels widely in the Protectorate with his work. He'll recognise these people, if he's ever seen them before. We were lucky he came into the Skyward this afternoon. A catch-up of old friends happened, with perfect timing: Damon, and Bill Sedley, and Geoff Dyer were all there, and are now enlisted in our ranks. Even Tom and Michael Frescombe, who stopped in for a quick one and found themselves drafted. I told them all about the man who's turned up and taken something that doesn't belong to him, and the fifteen-year-old boy who has been lied to. And the women, don't forget about the women, two of them, possibly victims, possibly slaves. The Protectorate stamps out that sort of thing. No, this can't wait for the local police to get their act together. Benny Sykes couldn't be found—was probably with one of his lady friends. Let's get down there and suggest they move on, that's all.

If Fosse told Dom about this apparent magic trick,

Dom didn't mention it when he turned up. In fact, he didn't say much of anything. We looked at each other, and I could see his fear for Fosse, as I'm certain he could see mine. We love that boy. We've never been closer, because of him.

That boy, safe at home, with instructions to not move, not to answer the door to anyone but us. Not until this is dealt with, one way or another.

I snap a broad stick from a branch and hold it tight.

We have a view over the farm. The man is visible. He has emerged from the barn and his face is raised to us; we're too far away to see his expression yet. He holds himself very still as we draw closer, weaving through the trees, I think he'll stand his ground to meet us on the farm's soil, feet planted, but then he starts walking towards us, briskly, and Dom is the one who stops and waits. The others come to a halt behind him, and we all wait. By the time the man has reached us he's got a smile prepared. He starts to speak and Dom interrupts him before he's through his first *hello*.

'Can I ask what you're doing here? This is private land.'

'Really?' The man raises one eyebrow. 'There was nobody here when we arrived. It was neglected, I would say.' He's tall and tanned, wearing a blue shirt and old ripped jeans. Attractive, and he knows it, but it won't help him with this crowd. His eyes take us all in. They slide over me, and move on. Yes, he probably thinks I'm the weak link. The woman. Perhaps he'll appeal to me directly, somehow. A sob story. But he turns his attention squarely on Dom, and I wonder if he won't try to play a different game altogether.

'Neglected or not, it's not your land,' says Dom.

'We've come from Liskeard way,' says the man. 'My name's Cee.' He holds out his hand.

'Time to move on,' says Dom.

'I'm from the Meadows' line of farmers down there. I'm looking for my own place, with my sisters. We've got years of experience between us—'

'Move on.'

Dom is solid. He knows all the tricks, every possible diversion into a different kind of argument, and he's keeping one fact dead ahead. Trespassing. Nothing justifies it. Nothing.

The others, though: will they waver? I've heard them talk long and late into the night about this being a place for local people first, even as Isley stands at the bar and serves them. But the Meadows family is well known around the Protectorate. They are a long line of farmers who expanded their business throughout the south, one of the first to accept trade and labour deals in lieu of money. It's a name that carries weight.

'We know what it means to be part of a place,' says Cee. He shifts his weight from one foot to the other, but he's keeping his arms apart, his body language open. A clever man. No wonder my son came to see him, maybe even trusted him to start with. But Fosse is clever too—he saw through it, eventually. 'We'd pay our way, as soon as we've got the place up and running. Give back. We wanted to come say hello properly once we were set up. I'm sorry it's come to this. It's my fault. But the lad said it would be better if I came bearing gifts, if you see what I mean. We were going to make baskets.'

'The land's spoken for,' says Dom, and I wince. That's a mistake.

'For who?' says Cee, so quick.

'Move on.'

'You want to give it to an outsider, I heard. Who ruled that? Were all of the council in agreement?'

'Move on,' Dom repeats, but it's losing its power.

Cee steps back. 'Of course. Give us a few days to get packed up, and we'll be on our way.'

Dom hesitates. From my position I can only see the back of his head, but I can imagine his expression. He's faltering. I can't watch him throw this all away. I hear myself say, 'No. Now,' and as soon as the words leave my lips, I know I've made the biggest mistake of this conversation. I shouldn't have talked. I've undermined our leader.

'Ah, now, surely a few days' grace is only reasonable,' says Cee, the voice very clear, and I can't counter him. I can't explain that I want him gone immediately so that the seeds of doubt he's trying to plant won't have time to grow. We never should have brought along the others; Dom and I should have come here ourselves. This isn't the kind of person who would go for trouble, confrontation, as his first move. The use of the magic trick to win Fosse over was evidence of that, but I wasn't paying attention. I'm an idiot.

'Two days,' says Dom.

'Four. That'll give us enough time to get packed up.'

'Three.'

Cee bows his head. 'Want to seal the deal with a drink? I have brew in the house.' How did he get that? Must be black market trade.

'Three days,' Dom repeats, and the others stand firm. At least I did something right; I promised them a free drink back at the Skyward after this was dealt with. Perhaps that's what's keeping them from returning his smile. I'd hate to think that was the only reason.

'Well, stop by any time if you change your mind. In the next three days, of course,' he adds. 'Good meeting you. This is fine land. It shouldn't lie fallow.'

Dom turns and walks away, past me, back through the trees. He doesn't look at me and he doesn't have to. I know he's furious with me, and I deserve it. Tom and the others follow after him, their eyes on the ground. They look like a bunch of boys rather than a wall of strength. How easily words, cleverly angled, can slip through the gaps in stones.

For a moment, I'm left alone with this man.

'You're his mother,' says Cee. 'Aren't you?'

'Stay away from him,' I say.

'Like you've been doing? He's a nice boy.' He starts back down to the farm.

He'll be gone in three days, I tell myself. He doesn't deserve a reply. I've already won.

'And for your next magic trick—fucking well disappear,' I call after him, and he doesn't look back, and I have lost. I'm ashamed of myself. I walk back to the Skyward feeling it. I part ways with Dom without a word and the rest of them lead the way back to the bar so I can serve them their free drinks, but they are subdued as they drink the brew down. They're thinking on what's been said and unsaid. They're still thinking by the time they leave, just after midnight, and I find myself closing up on my own and reaching for the only source of comfort that's ever really been there for me.

*　　*　　*

'YOU SHOULDN'T DO that,' he says.

I finish the last mouthful in the glass and turn it upside-down. I place it on my head. It's an old drinking game, from another time, when there was booze to waste.

'All gone,' I tell Isley.

'So I see.'

He comes to me, and sits on the stool with the cracked leather top. We've reversed our usual positions. I'm standing behind the bar, looking out over the dirty floor bearing the scuffle of muddy footprints, and the filled ashtrays of black-market cigarette butts, shipped over from Swansea.

'How did it go?' he asks me.

I shrug. If I start talking, I won't stop.

'I thought maybe it was a bad idea,' he muses.

That's true. That's what he said to me, when I went down to the cellar this afternoon and found him sitting beside Won, the two of them holding hands. He didn't seem guilty as he kept his grasp on her. I explained where I was going as quickly as I could, desperate to leave. She kept her eyes averted. He had frowned at me, at my explanation. *Fosse is in trouble*, I'd told him, and he had replied, *Trouble in what way? How can you be of help?* As if even the idea of it was ludicrous.

'You tried,' he says. 'I think that means something.'

'We dealt with it.'

'So what now?'

'Dom'll fill in Benny Sykes. He'll put together a team of specials and they'll check the farm in three days' time, to be certain they've gone. Then we'll all have a bit of a clean-up before the new family arrive. That's the plan.'

'I mean, what now for you and Fosse?'

'That's not your business,' I tell him. 'That's never been your business. Haven't I been clear about that from the beginning? What makes you think that's changed? You think because I'm drunk and you're not that you get to find out all my secrets?'

'Go to bed,' he says, and I have to touch him before he turns away from me. I reach for him, hold the sleeve of his shirt, and he flinches. His fingers are curved, as if protecting his palm.

'Have you hurt your hand?'

'It's fine. I caught it on a barrel.'

'Is it bad? Let me see.'

'Jem,' he says. 'Please don't.'

'You don't get to tell me what to do.'

'I never have!'

'Is Won ever leaving?' I ask, partially because I want to see how far I can push him, and partially because that's what I'm thinking. My control is slipping as the brew hits harder.

But it doesn't anger him. He leans forward, far over, and

lowers his head to the bar. He hits it with his forehead: once, twice, three times. Such a human action, born of exasperation. I can't help but smile. When he straightens up, he says, 'I've been perfectly clear that I don't like her being here either.'

'I saw you.'

'Saw me what?'

'Holding her hand.'

'Don't put stuff on it,' he says.

'What stuff?'

'Earth stuff.'

'Earth stuff?' The phrase tickles me. It fits, for all of this, for the people of the inn and the machinations of Dom and his cronies, for the confrontation today in the woods. You'd have to be human to care.

'Let's drink to Earth stuff,' I say, and I take up a fresh glass and the bottle of the very best. I pour out two measures—well, one and three quarters—and then the clay bottle is empty, and I say, 'You've got more of this, right?' Why is this funny? But he starts laughing, so I laugh too, and he takes the full glass and drains it.

'Right,' he says. 'Tell me what you're thinking. Tell me in the way only you can.'

The moment, the moment of capitulation, when the war is won. Or averted, we should say, and now I know exactly what I'm going to say.

*

The might of the Coalition gathers on Shanlingu. Many thousands of Qitans stand there, and face the forces of humanity down. I am not part of this. This is the first wave as I imagine it, from the pictures and footage I have seen.

The first wave was termed as exploratory, after initial investigations of the Kissing Gate had shown a fecund yet apparently uninhabited planet, rich with resources. The more I think about it, the more ridiculous it seems to think that anyone bought that lie at the time—how could the presence of intelligent life be completely overlooked? But, of course, we didn't—we, the Protectorate. We were the place that said *enough*, and parted ways with what used to be Great Britain as the deal was signed for the Coalition to make a new spaceport in Swansea. What used to be our island became a giant military base in no time at all. We watched and shook our heads as a first wave of thirty thousand soldiers arrived on Qita. Entirely peacefully, of course.

What a sight that must have been. I thought I'd been everywhere, leaving my leaflets, but the end of my tour approaches fast and it comes to me that there is still Shanlingu to see.

So I travel there, years after that one and only

confrontation, armed with my usual message of peace.

I have expectations of the land that are not met. It is not a vast and empty plain; at least, that's not all it is. It is a field, yes, covered in the kind of plant life that might remind a human of the wheat fields of home. But there's so much more to it: hillocks and muddy holes, and each plant is alive, just like on Earth, of course, but alive in a way that defies my complacency. How aware? Each movement of the orange stalk is strange. I crouch down and run one hand across them, and I could swear I *feel* the life in them. I will tread so carefully, with reverence, even though nobody died here. The Qitans welcomed us. The Coalition passed through. This was a war averted. Perhaps that's why I feel reverence. It's a space in which so many lives were saved; isn't that more holy than a massacre?

I take off my boots and socks, knot the strings and carry the boots around my neck as I start walking. Their weight is reassuring. I will walk the length of Shanlingu, carrying them and my backpack and all it means to be human and to be here. The plants will spring back under my feet with each step and we will all live.

There are no Qitans here. I wonder why not. What makes this place so different from the Zay Shines, say? Has anyone lived here since—the time of the fossils in the split rock of Toulu, say? Where does their history begin? There must be a record of it in the soil. Traces in the ground. What lies under the grassy plants? Bones and buildings. Or perhaps there is only a collective memory that does not need to be written down or rediscovered. I could ask you if that was true, but you won't tell me, I know, I know, you'll never tell me. I'm not meant to understand.

I walk for a long time. My feet are cold, and a light rain is falling, although the temperature is as mild as ever. There is still a vast expanse of open plain to go and I am hungry, but I won't eat here. It would feel like a transgression. I couldn't bear to drop one crumb of my Coalition-approved energy bar upon this land.

I walk on.

There must be many profound thoughts to think here, but I find myself recalling home instead. The Protectorate. The customs that people choose to preserve through sweat and effort.

My parents took Dom and I to Great Lington, once, to see a vast model of a church, built laboriously of wood. The townsfolk had spent all year constructing it. It was a replica, my mother told me. I didn't understand the word, whatever it was. *A copy*, Dom said. I asked where the original was, and he said: *gone*.

It was as big as a real church, this replica, and we all walked around it, slowly, solemnly, the townspeople and the tourists. *People come from all over*, said my father, not without disapproval. Then we were corralled into a small area of the green, behind a cordon. Only townsfolk were allowed to stay any closer than this. My father put me on his shoulders. He said: *watch*.

The mayor, in his polished chains and ermine finery, walked in a stiff, formal stride to the unreal church. He was handed a lit torch. The flame was bright, enticing in the approaching darkness of the evening; he put it to the church, and the church burned. It burned well and high as night fell, and we watched until the end, until there was nothing but ash. On the way back, in the car, when there was still petrol, Dom told me that the next day they'd start to build another church, just like the one before, like the original one that was blown up by Roundheads in the English Civil War. He'd been studying it in school.

We burn history down, over and over, as an act of remembrance. When there are no answers, there is recollection, and repetition.

But no, I won't give you my memories of Earth, of me. I promised myself. Qita, I give you Qita. The thick, grassy plants underfoot, and the end of the long walk as I reach the place where the pebbles start, and proliferate, and then there is hard rock, and the mountains begin. I can see a settlement in the distance, up a white path against the purple rise. It reminds me of my duty. I put my socks and boots back on, and then I take an extendable pole from my backpack and drive it into one of the rocks. I attach a leaflet to the pole.

There are two Qitans standing not far away, on an outcropping. They watch me, and they do not move. I summon my landcruiser with my wrist control, and as I wait for its arrival I look back over the plain once more. Each plant, so alive, moving like the hair of some creature, or a sea of wiggling fingers. And when I look down to the rock, there is liquid welling up from the place where the pole penetrated; I have wounded the land. And this is no longer just land, but the body, the body of my son that I have stabbed, and he lies there with the pole rising up from his stomach, the leaflet attached, and then looks at me with such confusion as he says: *I'm alone*

No, no, no, this isn't happening, that isn't what happened, and I shut my mouth tight and refuse to speak, I will not stand here and bear that look on his face or on yours. I have done my best. That has to mean something. I leave the bar, and head for bed.

'Please,' Isley calls to me as I climb the stairs. 'Please.' I don't know what he's asking for.

* * *

FOSSE CLENCHED AND unclenched his hands.

He had outgrown his room. When he lay in his single bed, he had to bend his knees to keep his feet from poking out from under the duvet, hanging in empty space. His possessions looked smaller and less meaningful to him: the eagle feather in the frame on his wall; the multicoloured plastic tub that had once held ice cream and had lived on his windowsill for years; inside that, the collection of old coins marked with a Queen's head; the new and old atlases, side by side on his shelf. His clothes looked so shrunken that he was surprised to find he could still fit in them every morning.

You don't have to stay in your room, his uncle had said. But he had a strong suspicion that if he left, he wouldn't be able to squeeze back in, and it was ridiculous, he knew that: it belonged to him. It would always accommodate him. He was so angry at himself for thinking things had changed, that he had changed, and very afraid that he was making it true.

He never thought he'd miss going to school, but being kept at home for a few days made Fosse aware that school offered a quiet, resilient shape to his day. It let him come and go, in the main: a haven when he needed it that demanded little in return. Now he could glimpse what the end of his time at school might be like, and he wanted to return and be grateful of its walls and schedules for a little while, at least, before the feeling wore off.

His uncle hadn't given him a timescale for staying home, and wouldn't say exactly what had happened at the farm. He'd said something about it being dealt with, about them leaving, and then asked the question:

Do you want to spend more time with your mum?

There had followed a number of questions and comments that felt like a tentative groping towards some central hole of accusation. But Fosse could not fill that hole; the words would not come. It was not a matter of preference but necessity that had made him choose to tell his mother of the farm. He had needed a particular kind of relationship to reveal the truth—he couldn't care too much about the person he told, but had to be sure they would care enough about him to act on his behalf. And it helped that he planned to stop seeing his mother in the future, so that he didn't have to bear the knowing looks in her eyes. He recoiled from the absolute horror of the idea that she knew him, had seen him in a new light, because of this event. That she had come to see how he was, deep inside: corrupted. Better to never look at her again.

He could not stop looking at his hands.

They, too, could no longer be trusted. His own hands had given him no reason to doubt them yet, but he couldn't forget what he'd seen. Hands that had merged and emerged. Nobody else could solve this part of the puzzle, not his mother, not his uncle. His mother had not really taken in what he had told her beyond the obvious at all, he thought. There had been part of the story that she had clung to and acted upon: *my son is in danger*. He despised how much she had enjoyed hearing that he needed her.

He couldn't even bear to touch himself. He suspected that was why he was so angry. There was no release open to him, not since the magic trick and the graveyard. The fear created a strong image in his mind, of stroking himself and his hand sinking, melding, creating a hot fused mess of his own intimate flesh. He dreamed of the barn. It had been such a clear, fine space of his own, and he had been wide open within it, his legs bare, free in the fresh air. And the axe, the swinging of the axe. The thought of its handle and the sharp curve of the blade was nearly enough to soothe him, but then he thought of Annie, soft and doughy, the axe sinking between her breasts in his imagination, her hands held up to stop him, and his desire would ebb away.

Annie was leaving, along with Victoria. And Cee. They would leave soon, if they hadn't gone already. The walls of his room were so much smaller. The bed would hardly hold his weight.

'Fosse! Time to go.'

To Schillings Barn, for the weekly meeting. He had

nearly forgotten, or had imagined he might be exempt this time. He sat up, and thought about calling down the stairs that he didn't want to go. But then he remembered that Mrs Satterly would be there, and he wanted to see her. To look at her hands.

'Coming!' he called.

It was strange to think he would never fit back in this room. When would that moment come, the door refusing to admit him, the bed no longer holding his weight? He took care to leave the room casually, without a backward glance. He did not want to think so hard that he made his thoughts true.

Minutes for Council Meeting 30th October

Request box delay as Mr Samuels unable to work due to illness.

School to take surplus apples and make sauce for Homecraft lessons.

Requests sorted and discussed. It was agreed to look into how much resurfacing the children's play area would cost as one of the Trench twins had an accident and sprained her ankle in a muddy puddle.

Reverend Sumner made a joke about disaster zones, then promised to say a prayer for the Trench child on Sunday. She reported that Church attendance is low and suggested a fete. Council to discuss at the next meeting.

Higher Council Business: No non-essential permits to be given to travel outside of Protectorate land until the quarantines have been lifted. The arrival of the new farming family for Valley Farm has therefore been delayed. No new date set.

Urgent Coalition/Protectorate meeting on quarantines and rising incidents of illness called in Bristol on 3rd November. An attendee is needed from the village. To be decided.

AOB: Warning—criminals operating in the area, possible smuggling taking place, any sign of stolen material to be confiscated and returned to the council.

Mrs Satterly requests vet treatment for her dog Bailey, possible trade options? Discussion was held about the location of the nearest vet since the quarantine has been extended to Barnstaple.

Meeting ended.

* * *

'THANK YOU SO much,' said Mrs Satterly, again, as she led the way to her front room and began to light the candles above the fireplace. The room was cold and felt unused to Fosse; he couldn't picture her sitting in here in the evenings, not on her own, when two armchairs were arranged before the fire so carefully. This was a room for a couple. If the ghost of Mr Satterly had been anywhere, it would have been here. Not at the graveyard at all.

But there was Bailey.

'He's not getting up from his basket,' she said.

Poor Bailey, fat and tired, making an effort to wag and managing only two soft thumps of his tail on the floor when Fosse knelt beside him. No dog could look both as sad, and happy, as a Labrador, he thought. The eyes opened, and the long fine hairs extending from the eyebrows lifted, quivered, before the eyes slowly shut again. The chest heaved.

'Bailey,' he said. As soon as Mrs Satterly had arrived at the Schilling Barn without the dog in tow, Fosse had known something was wrong.

'I'm certain he's just under the weather,' she said. She'd been repeating herself a lot since the meeting, and this was one of her favourite phrases. The more she said it, the less believable it sounded. She had taken to it like a mantra, a spell, a prayer.

'Hello, boy,' said his uncle.

'Mint tea, Dominic?'

'Yes, please, Freya.'

Off she went to the kitchen, with purpose, and his uncle knelt down beside him and touched the top of Bailey's head. It gave Fosse the courage to touch the dog too. He ran his hand across Bailey's shoulder; the fur felt different. Coarser.

His uncle shook his head, and said very quietly, 'Not sure anyone will travel with this quarantine business, but perhaps a vet couldn't help anyway. Bailey's just old, you know?'

How easy it was, then, to give up fighting for a life. His uncle was well-armed with reasons: age, distance, and, after all, this was only a dog. Should they simply wait for the dog to die? If it were that easy, what was the difference between that and living?

'We have to help him,' said Fosse.

'I know it's hard, mate.'

'Don't *manage* me!' he snapped, and heard his mother in his words. Could anything ever be escaped? 'We have to try.'

His uncle sighed, and reached out to the dog again. This time he ran his hands over the head, then the neck, then the chest. He brushed over Fosse's hand and continued down to the stomach to push, probe the skin there. Bailey bore it with patience.

Mrs Satterly said from the doorway, 'How do you want it?' Fosse hadn't even heard her come back in.

'Just a drop of cold water, please,' said his uncle. His hands didn't stop their exploration.

'Fosse?'

'No, thank you,' he said automatically.

'I know how he feels,' she said, looking sadly at the dog. 'Sometimes I don't want to get up any more either. But I'm certain he's just a bit under the weather, really.'

His uncle examined the curled hips, the back legs, then the paws. Bailey flinched and bared his teeth, then tried to shift away. 'All right, boy. Fosse, can you just hold his collar, just in case?'

'Oh, he'd never hurt you,' said Mrs Satterly.

Fosse held the dog's neck still, sliding his fingers under the old leather collar.

'Hmmm,' said his uncle. 'Okay. Okay.'

'What is it?' Mrs Satterly loomed over them, blocking the candlelight.

'Could you just stand back for a minute? Thanks. It's just a tender spot, I think. Yes. It's sore, boy. Yes, I see.'

Bailey made an effort to snap at his uncle. The strength behind it surprised Fosse. This was not a failing dog, after all. He still had fight in him. Perhaps this was something that could be fixed. He could hear that possibility in his uncle's voice, too, energised as he said, 'Have you got some old socks, Freya?'

'Socks?'

'And some string. Could you fetch them for me?'

'Well, I—yes, I...' Off she went, muttering to herself.

'What is it?' said Fosse.

'Listen, I'm not certain. I just think maybe we can at least make him more comfortable if we try this, but I'm not promising anything.' When Mrs Satterly returned with the socks and string he set to work at speed, wrapping up Bailey's paws and tying the socks in place.

'There we go,' he said.

The dog stopped trying to see what was happening. Fosse let go of his collar and he lay still. Then he stretched out all four legs and pulled himself upright. He stepped from his basket and shook himself, then set off across the room in the direction of the kitchen.

'Well I never,' said Mrs Satterly, and the three of them followed the dog and gathered in the kitchen doorway to watch him eat the entire contents of his food bowl. Then he took long, slurping mouthfuls of water, standing there in his floppy socks tied up with string.

'Ha-haaaa!' said his uncle, and clapped Fosse on the back. Fosse felt such relief that he hugged both of them, and enjoyed them clasping him in return. A problem solved; problems could be solved: the worst things didn't always have to happen. Life was not just the business of waiting to die.

'His paws are sensitive,' said his uncle. 'He doesn't like the feel of them on the floor. They must be very tender.'

'Why would that have happened?' asked Mrs Satterly, then burst into tears. Fosse hugged her again, tight, and let her pour herself out on him. He felt covered by her burst grief, drenched in it. 'It's my fault,' she said. 'It's my fault.'

'Why would that be?' said his uncle. 'Come on, now.'

She cried on until Bailey finished his drink and came to stand in front of her, and then she hugged the dog instead, who bore it with what looked to Fosse like resignation. Then he set off back to the front room, choosing to lie by the unlit fire instead.

'Yes, right, a fire,' said Mrs Satterly. 'Coming right up. You drink your tea and I'll get one going. It's a cold night, isn't it? Wintery. Haven't felt one like it in years.'

His uncle returned to the living room in the wake of Mrs Satterly, and Fosse followed reluctantly. She knelt by the fireplace and started to arrange logs in the grate, slowly, using only her left hand.

'Freya,' said his uncle. Fosse knew that tone well.

'It's all right,' said Mrs Satterly. 'It's from the graveyard.

I didn't ever think it would bother Bailey.' She didn't turn around, continued with her task. 'The ground is so soft out there, and I, well, I put my hand in. I've been doing it every night. We've been holding hands. But then Bailey wanted to dig there, and I let him. Just a little bit. Not far down. I know it was wrong, but it was a comfort, I think, it was a comfort.'

'Can I see your hand?' his uncle said.

'No, I don't think I want you to do that.'

There was an uncomfortable silence. His uncle wasn't used to not getting his own way, but Mrs Satterly's curved back was a wall he could not penetrate, and she would not turn around for him.

'Will you let Doctor Clarke take a look at it?' said his uncle.

'Yes, yes, I can see Doctor Clarke, yes.'

'Yes, please. Can you make an appointment in the morning?'

'Yes, yes, I'll do that, Dominic, yes.'

'Okay. Right.' His uncle put down the tea, unfinished, and Fosse followed suit. 'Keep Bailey in for a few days, Freya, and we can talk about this more later, all right? I'll come back tomorrow, after you've seen the doctor.'

'Yes, fine, lovely.' She was babbling, and the way she followed them both to the door made Fosse feel certain she was keen to get rid of them. The soft soil, the image of her and Bailey scrabbling in the mud, was so strong in his mind. And the magic trick was mixed in with his thoughts: Cee, and Annie, and Victoria all merging into one another. Hands.

'Let's just swing by the graveyard,' said his uncle, as Mrs Satterly's door closed. Fosse felt a wild surge of gladness and terror. He had been wrong about death; the fact was that nothing wanted to die any more. Nothing was done with, and nothing could be left behind.

THE SOIL WAS the same: soft, like jelly. Undisturbed. Mrs Satterly had made the whole thing up, then. Or could the ground have returned to its smooth state? Settled back to apparent normality? It was too disturbing to imagine.

'Keep the torch on it,' said his uncle.

Fosse aimed the beam squarely on the spot in front of the young cherry tree. The beam was weak, flickering.

'When's the last time you charged that up? You know it's one of your jobs.'

'Sorry.'

He could hear the tension in his uncle's voice as he touched the soil and said, 'It surely couldn't have...' A ripple rolled out from his finger, like water. Not like water: the concentric circles did not return to his uncle's finger, but froze in place, and a dent in the middle formed and deepened, and then slowly, so slowly, the soil moved back into position to create a flat surface once more.

A noise, in the trees, on the left—a sudden fluttering. Fosse jumped, and the torch beam skittered off target.

'A bird,' said his uncle.

'Yeah.' He swung the beam back in place, and there was no way to tell that anything had disturbed the earth at all.

'It's a kind of mud.' His uncle let out a breath, and said, 'Maybe a water pipe's burst underneath it. Although surely, we all would have lost water pressure through the village, if that had happened. Or it could be a new underground river, forming, you know, there's so much more ground water around, what with all the rain…'

It hadn't really rained for months, though. A dry autumn: Fosse had heard one of the teachers at school saying that. But he didn't give voice to it. Then his brain insisted on reminding him that it would be Halloween tomorrow, and he told himself: *shut up shut up that's not even a real thing anyway*. Halloween, when graveyards come to life and the dead rise, and usually the kids went out in the village in costume, door to door, knocking for small treats. He did it last year, pretending to be ironically detached with a black cape and a pair of fangs cut out of cardboard, but he wouldn't do it this year. He'd never do it again.

'Should I put up a sign saying the graveyard is out of bounds for now?' said his uncle, mainly to himself, Fosse suspected. 'That won't be popular.' He gave out another long sigh. Fosse couldn't remember ever seeing him so stuck for answers. 'What I don't understand is how it could have affected both dog skin and human skin.'

Fosse shrugged.

The fluttering noise again, then a small sound, high-pitched, maybe a whine, and he swung the torch to it once more, expecting to see Mr Satterly standing there, watching them from behind the trunk of a tree. But there was nothing. The trunk was a white line against the darkness, and the whine was coming from his own mouth. He forced himself to be silent.

'God, I'm sorry, mate,' said his uncle, 'Sorry, I should have thought, after all you've been through. Look, shine the torch down here and look the other way, okay? I won't touch it. I just want to look carefully at it.'

He returned the beam to the grave and obediently turned his face away, in the direction of the gate. His uncle huffed out a sharp breath. Fosse strained to hear every movement. He waited, and waited. Something was rising. The thing, whatever it was, the thing that would change everything. A scream, a horror, a terror worthy of Halloween. A body crawling up, crawling forth, grabbing his uncle, dragging him down.

'Okay,' said his uncle. 'Let's go.'

They walked through the graves to the gate. This time around, it wasn't the names Fosse noticed, but the tokens of remembrance. The dry remains of flowers from the summer, but also small trinkets and carved wooden symbols, potted plants, and twists of shiny paper. One bore a jam jar containing silver coins. Once, maybe, they had belonged to the person buried there. This was now their allocated space, and they could never outgrow it, could they? If he died here, his own coin collection would be placed atop the small rectangle of land bearing his name, and someone might say:

They might say:

There was nothing to say about him.

Then the fear started, and he knew he couldn't bear to go back to that bedroom again. He was bursting, he had to be free, and he took off at a sprint, leaving his uncle in the dark, his heart hammering in the hope that he was not too late to find a way out, to cut up and out—through the village, first, across the green with the houses quiet, the shops black, onwards, past the school, and his feet found the route he knew so well that he didn't need the faint, flickering torchlight. But then he thought of Cee's plan to make deadly pits and he slowed as he reached the fields to come to a halt on the cusp of the woods. Would Cee really have laid his traps? It was no good: he couldn't go back. Only forward.

He tested each step with his toes before daring to plant his feet. It took so long, and he was afraid his uncle would find him—even heard him calling out, he thought, but the sound seemed far away and unreal. Eventually Fosse reached the crest of the hill. A soft yellow glow came from the windows of the farmhouse below, and smoke wound from the chimney.

He was not too late.

VICTORIA OPENED THE door; the naked suspicion on her face fell into shock.

'Hi,' Fosse said.

'What are you doing here?'

Cee appeared behind her, and pulled her back. She hovered behind him, her arms crossed over her stomach. 'Fucking hell,' he said. He leaned on the door jamb. 'Didn't expect to see you again.'

'I thought you might be gone,' Fosse said. 'I ran here, well, I ran as far as—'

'We're not going anywhere.'

'But my uncle said—'

'We've got more right to this farm than anyone. We're

staying. We know what to do with the place, the land.'

'The new people coming in are farmers,' said Fosse, miserably; he had wanted them to be leaving, he knew that from the disappointment he felt. He had wanted to go with them. Now that seemed like an impossibility, as much from Cee's manner as his words. Fosse's lips were very dry. He licked them, and asked, 'Is Annie there?'

'She's ill.'

'Can I see her?' He wanted to be inside the farmhouse with her, to make it like it was before.

Cee said nothing. Victoria asked, tentatively, one hand on Cee's shoulder, 'Maybe he should come in? It's a cold night.'

'No, maybe he shouldn't fucking come in,' said Cee, his voice soft. 'He picked a side.'

So there were sides, and Fosse had picked one without knowing it, and Cee had decided he was the enemy.

'Did you make those pits? The ones you were talking about?' he asked. He glanced at the wood pile by the door. The pile of sticks he had helped to chop had shrunk. The axe was there. The head was buried in the flat trunk, and the red handle pointed towards his hand.

'Maybe you should get on home now,' said Victoria.

'Where's Annie?' He couldn't go without seeing her.

'I'm here.' Her voice came from inside the farmhouse, high and thin. 'Hold on.'

Fosse waited. So did Cee and Victoria, unmoving, until she appeared behind them. Then they parted and let her through, taking care not to touch her. She looked very tired, moving as if her joints and muscles hurt, bending at the waist. He was so much younger than her. He'd never really noticed that before.

'What's wrong?' he said.

'Nothing, love, you should go home.' She stood outside in the cold with him, and she did not seem to feel it. 'Be careful, going back through the woods.' She glanced at Cee, but he said nothing.

Fosse hesitated, then said, 'Come with me.'

'Come where? Walk you back to your house, you mean?'

'No. Away.'

'Are you a fucking idiot?' said Cee.

'I can't go away with you, Fosse. I'm sorry. You need to go home and forget all about this, all right?'

'I can't.'

'Yes, yes, you can. Your uncle's a good man. He'll understand. A good family always understands.'

'Yeah, you should sew that on to a cushion,' said Cee, squinting at them both. 'This is hilarious. Why don't we go home too? Oh, that's right, we can't, because the council closed up the border and told us we were diseased, remember? We thought we'd be better off on our own, didn't we? Remember that discussion?'

'It might have reopened by now,' said Victoria.

'You think it's all better? Annie, what do you think?'

She shook her head.

'Is this about the quarantines?' Fosse asked.

Cee stared at him. 'What do you know about that?'

'Barnstaple's closed off, my uncle said.'

'That's not far away,' said Victoria. 'It's getting closer.'

He was so cold, and yet still had no idea of where he could go, what he could do. He wanted to be indoors, even if it was with Cee. He wanted to win them all back over to liking him. 'Can I come in?' he asked. 'Just to get warm.'

'You don't want to do that,' said Annie. 'We're not well.'

'What's the matter?'

Cee held up his left hand. 'Turns out it's not a magic trick after all,' he said, in a sing-song voice. 'Annie.'

She didn't respond. Her own hands stayed tucked in the long sleeves of her jumper.

'Annie,' Cee commanded, again.

Let's go, Fosse wanted to say, so badly. *Let's go now.*

She lifted her arm, and the sleeve fell back to reveal her hand.

The skin on her knuckles moved first. It tented, lifting from the bone, straining towards the door. To Cee. Annie grabbed her wrist and held her hand still, and the skin stretched itself further, from the tips and joints of her fingers; all of the skin was trying to pull itself free from her hand to his. Fosse thought it would rip. He couldn't bear to see it, but he didn't look away.

'It's doing it on its own,' Annie said. Her voice was mild, curious. There was no pain in it. Victoria retreated into the house, her own hands behind her back. 'It gets harder to stay apart. It wants us to stay stuck together.'

'She's got it the worst,' said Cee. 'Look at her arm.' The skin around her left wrist, between the grip of her fingers, was bulging outwards, filled with its own purpose. 'They think a quarantine's going to stop it, but we know what comes next.'

So this was the disease.

'What comes next?' Fosse whispered.

'Don't tell him lies,' said Annie. 'You don't know.'

'I've heard things.'

'You don't know!'

'Everyone'll get it eventually. Have you checked your hand? It always starts in the hand.'

'No,' said Fosse.

'Show me.' Cee reached out, grabbed at him. Annie said, 'Don't, Cee, don't,' and he pushed past her. Fosse wanted to ask for help, but he couldn't speak—it was always the same, when he needed to, he couldn't speak and Cee was nearly touching him, the skin of the hand pulling, stretching. Annie started forwards; Cee would hurt her; he would hurt them all. Fosse took up the axe. The weight of it gave him strength; he planted his feet, as he had done in the field, so many times, and felt his body move, muscle memory taking over. He lifted it overhead and swung it down.

The blade sank into Cee's shoulder. Fosse felt the collar bone break as it sheared through.

Cee crumpled under the weight of it, sank to his knees. He *could* be beaten. A surge of fear and triumph took over, and Fosse used it to pull the axe free: it took all his strength. Blood shot up, gushed from the slice he had made in Cee's body. It was everywhere, so fast, all over Cee's face, all over the wood and the door and the ground, and Annie too, who stood there, not moving, not seeing. Cee's head tilted back to the sky and his eyes rolled upwards. The blood sprayed and pooled and did not stop. He toppled backwards and lay with his chest heaving, his arms flung out to the sides. The fingers of his left hand squirmed, like worms, each one moving independently. They looked as if they were trying to break free of the body and burrow down to safety. Fosse thought of how worms could be cut and yet go on living—was that true? He couldn't remember if it was true or not. He lifted the axe and brought it down again, this time on Cee's hand, where the fingers met the palm. It was a well-aimed blow, severing them all. They wriggled for a moment more, then stopped moving.

Fosse felt a shaft of pain in his palm. He dropped the axe, stared at his hand, but it was not the disease. A large splinter had stuck there, from the red handle, jammed deep into his skin. He looked to the doorway. Victoria and Annie watched him, eyes wide, wary.

He said, 'What do I do?' It was as close as he could get to saying *help me*.

Victoria came out of the house and knelt beside Cee, her knees in the pool of blood. Blood kept spurting from the wound in the shoulder, and she put her hands over it. 'Cee,' she said.

Annie said, 'Go.'

'Where?'

'He didn't mean it,' she said, 'He wants you to be with us. He thought you could be with us.'

Could she not come with him, hold him together somehow? But hitting Cee had shattered that illusion; he had never been seeing her clearly. She would only talk of Cee, because she had chosen her side before she even came to the farm. And there was her hand, too. He couldn't bear her hand. Her sleeve had fallen down, covering it. Her eyes were so wide.

'I wouldn't ever hurt you,' he said.

'Go!' Stronger, this time, and her eyes were fixed on his. He obeyed so he wouldn't have to face her gaze, but he wanted so strongly to please her, to make things better, even as he ran away. Then he remembered her instruction from earlier—before the thing he had just done with the axe that he didn't really understand yet, not yet—and slowed, took his time through the woods. He walked with slow deliberate care, testing each step of the way. He couldn't have disobeyed her if his life depended on it.

Go! she had said.

It was dawn when he reached Wrecker's Cave, found a woman and three men unloading crates there, and traded his good watch for passage to Swansea.

IT'S BEEN THE longest of nights.

They would not go home, and there was a desperate edge to their drinking. We're running low on brew: not just the good stuff, but all of it. Isley has stopped making batches. He never leaves the cellar any more.

'They getting all loved up down there?' asked Simon Lane, and they all laughed. I laughed along. Nobody complained about the lack of food tonight. I've given up trying to cobble together a menu and serve at the same time. At this rate I reckon we have maybe two days before we run dry, and I don't care. I don't care about anything but Fosse and Dom.

I went over to the house this morning. Nothing had changed. Nothing was missing. They didn't pack. They didn't even tidy; a plate sat in the sink, bearing crumbs, a smear of chutney. I went from the house to find Benny Sykes, and I reported them missing. He wondered aloud if they weren't off on official council business somewhere, or maybe camping. I asked him if he knew many people that went camping in November, and got a patient gaze in return.

I know everyone thinks I gave up all rights to my son, long ago. I understand that. That's why nobody will listen if I speak of my mother's instinct telling me that something is wrong. I wouldn't believe it myself, except I'm not the only one that knows it.

It's not just Fosse and Dom. It's everywhere. The feeling of wrongness. Every customer forces their laughs and drinks too fast, and none of them want to say why.

I promised myself I wouldn't go down to the cellar any more. They sit so close together. But I can't help myself tonight. I need him. If I can't speak to him, then I am utterly alone. I thought that was what I wanted, once; to be alone. I sought it out, far away. But it turns out that the only place in which I could ever be truly alone is right here, back where I started. Alone is not a place I can go to, but the place that's left behind after everyone else has gone.

I take the steps slowly.

Won is asleep. Her head rests on Isley's shoulder, tucked into the crook of his neck. They are holding hands, of course. He is awake, but from the way he blinks I can tell he's very tired. The last of his bruises from the attack have faded.

'Already?' he says, very quietly.

It makes no sense. What does he know? I say, 'Something's happened.'

'I can show you.'

'Fosse and Dom are missing,' I say, then, 'What?'

'I can show you,' he repeats. 'What happened. What comes next. But I don't want to, I swear I never wanted to.'

'You know what's happened.'

'I told you to watch him.'

'I did my best,' I say, 'You know what's happened to Fosse? Where is he?'

'You did your best,' Isley says. Why does that sound so terrible? It's not as if anyone can do more than their best, and yet it feels like an excuse. Isley can tell. I should have been more than I am, capable of more, from the very start. I should have forced Fosse to accept me when I came back from Qita. There should have been a way.

'You could have helped me, if you knew something was wrong, instead of hiding away down here with your girlfriend.' It comes out loud, an accusation, but Won does not wake up. Isley shifts his weight and her head moves with him. She is stuck to him. He lifts his hand and hers comes with it. They are glued together, and I don't think there's even skin separating them, not in the places where they touch. They are bleeding together.

'I knew it was stupid,' says Isley. 'To even try to stay separate. But you made me think it was possible. You've been so contained. I wanted that.' He holds out his free hand to me. 'I love you, you know that, right?'

'We love each other,' I whisper.

'I can help you, now. Before it all falls down.'

'How?'

'Look at your hand.'

It feels normal. But when I hold it up, I can see that the skin is alive and moving, stretching itself towards Isley's hand. It is elastic, pulling itself as far from the bones as it can. It wants to be with him.

'I can tell you what happens to Fosse,' he says. 'You won't know, otherwise. You'll never know. It's a free choice, on your part. I know you're scared.'

'Tell me where he is now,' I say, watching my skin reach for him.

'It doesn't work that way. We have to touch. It's like…'

He pauses, tilts his head, and I see him so clearly in the movement. He's still Isley, and I trust him, and love him, as I have for years. '…it's like telling a story. Just like the stories you've told. We had to be together for the story to grow.'

I can't do it. I'm too afraid of what's happening. Of the way Won is melting into him. But if I don't, I'll never know where my son is. Could that be true? Would Isley lie to me?

'It's not forever,' Isley sighs. He closes his eyes. 'Just a taste. To see where he's gone.'

Just a taste.

All I've ever wanted is to hold his hand.

I step forward.

I take his hand.

PART FIVE

Supply Movements.

Crowd Control.

Logistics.

An intensive training course followed the results of the On-Board Evaluation. Also a special diet, to build his muscles. When they asked him if he objected to an implant on religious grounds, being one of those rare recruits from the Protectorate, he said he didn't. He needed to be different, different from before, and accepting the implant was the quickest way to achieve that.

Even so, it wasn't until after Fosse had completed one whole cycle of work at Tung Base—the flight through the Kissing Gate to Qita already fading from his mind—

that he began to trust that his new, powerful body and augmented mind could not possibly have anything to do with the boy he had been.

He had become a man.

A retinal display of tasks and navigational aids took care of his thoughts in work mode, and he found this augmentation fascinating enough to make the time pass quickly. When he clicked into leisure mode, the Coach took over, making a playground of the mind that he could not resist. Everything took on a brightly coloured element of fun that scored him points in key categories from social skills to personal hygiene; the points could then be traded for further upgrades.

Fosse liked to turn his pod into different Earth environments, and each one was utterly real to him as long as he did not try to move within them. He lay on his cot amongst the lush, verdant trees and insect clicks of the Amazon estate, or rode a hot air balloon over the folds and turns of the Great Wall preservation. He enjoyed Antarctica's deep blue sky above and seeded ice below, and even slept at the heart of the Forestal complex of Southern France.

The only time he came across an environment that felt false was when the boy managed to sneak past the man, and he explored the virtual soil of the Western Protectorate. It only happened once, and he knew within a moment of arriving there that it was a flawed copy. He stood in a farmyard and smelled fresh straw. A bird tweeted a musical tune. A shiny tractor was parked next to a farmhouse; the door was ajar, and an apple pie was visible on the table within. The hand of the digital designer had been dipped in nostalgia for a place that had never existed.

Fosse had logged out, and when Coach asked him to rate the experience, he'd given it one star out of five. Then he'd gone to his desk, opened the drawer, and taken out the splinter from the axe that had planted itself in his skin that night. He'd dug it out of his palm on the boat trip over from Swansea, using the pain to distract him from his seasickness and his terror. He hadn't been able to part with it since. It represented a truth about himself, a truth that Coach could not cover, or augment.

From then on, he stuck to places he could believe in, having nothing in his head with which to compare them.

AFTER A LONG shift of relocating crates from one ship to another—a last-minute change in destination due to a maintenance issue—Fosse hit the gym, asking Coach to overlay it with the Circus augmentation. He was lifting extreme weights on a tightrope for a sea of impressed onlookers within a red silk tent when a soft chime in his ear informed him that reality was trying to get his attention.

He put away the circus, then the weights, and faced a man in an immaculate suit. Not military, then—one of the private contractors.

'Fosse Davey? I'm Li Zhou. Human Relations. I provide a personal interface service between Tung's Coach users here on Qita and the designers back on Earth. Do you have time for an informal conversation?' He spoke English well, and his eyes were noticeably blue. Could they be the next stage in implants? Fosse wondered what else Zhou was seeing. Fosse's own implant only displayed the name in small letters at the edge of his vision. No other details were forthcoming; the firewall of rank was firmly in place. It was an option for lower ranks to pay for their own privacy, but Fosse had no idea why a person would want that.

'About what?'

'I'd love to know your thoughts in regard to a particular matter. I have a room booked, if that's acceptable?'

'Fine,' said Fosse. He picked up his towel and left behind his uniform, suspecting the politeness was only a cover for whatever came next. Could they have found out about Cee? Just the thought of it made him feel sick, but he pushed those feelings down deep as Zhou made small talk with him, walking by his side.

They made their way to the inner circle of the base—a section Fosse didn't have clearance to enter unaccompanied—and the Human Relations division. The open spaces of the loading and clerical areas gave way to smaller and smaller glass-walled sections, then to opaque white walls and hard metal doors at regular intervals. Zhou opened a door with silver characters, in many languages, stretching from the top to the handle, and Fosse followed him into a very small cube of an office, one wall of which featured a projection of a coastal megacity, possibly an old one; he'd noticed a strong trend for nostalgia in the images selected for display around the base.

He took a seat on one side of a small square table, and Zhou took the one opposite. It felt confrontational.

'You gave the Western Protectorate augmentation one star,' said Zhou.

'Yes.'

'You came from there.'

'Yes.'

'Your natural upbringing means we only have basic records for you.' Fosse had come across the word a few times now; it meant a childhood with no access to computer technology. The concept surprised, even shocked, people who hadn't considered there was any other way to live any more, and the questions he had been asked about it by his workmates was one of the reasons why he'd kept himself to himself whenever he could. Zhou tapped the tabletop twice, then traced a complex shape upon it. 'Did you grow up living in a house, can I ask?'

'Yes,' said Fosse.

'Within a purely rural environment?'

Could a house ever be in a purely rural place? 'I don't understand the question,' he said. 'It was part of a village. An estate on the edge of the village, but a lot of people had moved out.'

'You farmed your own fruit and vegetables?'

'Some of them.'

'Raised and slaughtered animals?'

The question made him angry. He said, 'Not personally, no. Do you do that yourself?'

'I'm sorry,' said Zhou, tracing more characters on the tabletop, 'Forgive all these questions.' He sat back in his chair. 'Ridiculous, I know. I'll tell you what this is regarding. The Rural Dynamic Team for the Coach system is a prestigious area of work for programmers. They pride themselves on a good result. So your response to the Protectorate augmentation caused quite a response back there, and they asked me to contact you directly to discuss the matter. It's very concerning to them that they've got it wrong, you see.'

'They've looked at my ratings?'

'Of course.' So that was why some people paid for privacy from Coach. Still, it was the truth. The augmentation wasn't realistic. It couldn't be a mistake to tell them so, when they asked for the ratings. The teachers at school had used to say that feedback could be the best tool for becoming a better person.

Zhou looked earnest in his assumed informality. *Imagine*, thought Fosse, *this is his pride and joy, this job is his life. Imagine having a job that takes up your whole life.* It was the thought of hurting Zhou's feelings, oddly, that made Fosse temper his words. 'It's not wrong, exactly, but it's not how I remember it.'

'Is that not the same thing?' said Zhou.

'I don't think so.'

'You think the augmentation is better or worse than your memory of it?'

Fosse couldn't answer that. 'Different,' he said.

'Could you describe how? I can give you a visual prompt.' He traced his finger on the tabletop once more, and a woodland glade, dappled sunlight through green leaves, replaced the coastal cityscape. There was nothing of the Protectorate about it. Everything was different: the air, the leaves, the birdsong. He could sense where the edges lay. At home there was so much land to walk upon, to run from, yet with it, the knowledge that it was also small, in the ways that mattered. It had a finite quality, originating from the ways things had lived and died in it. In the fact that, on Protectorate soil, he had attacked someone—maybe killed them, maybe a murderer, no, not to think of that—but in that picture everything was clean and new and blameless.

The silence lasted for quite a while, beyond the point of embarrassment. Eventually Zhou traced a finger, and the image was replaced with a blank wall. 'I'm sorry,' he said. 'I should have checked your profile more carefully. Your aptitude tests show you have minimal ability to respond verbally to questions. The fault is mine. Please accept my apologies.'

'No, I—it's only that I—' He felt his cheeks quivering, tears threatening. He put the heels of his palms to his eyes and willed the boy in him away. How could he have been classified so easily, that information placed within computers to be seen by whomever had the clearance to look? What else did it say about him?

'Your memories of the Protectorate—upset you?'

'Yes,' he said, shortly, incapable of more.

'It's not uncommon,' said Zhou, kindly. 'Ask sickbay for a hazer. It won't alter your memories, but it will make them less... intense for you. Homesickness can be a serious problem if not treated. I can make you a priority appointment, if that suits? There, it's done. Go along whenever you're ready.'

'Thank you,' said Fosse. He got up to leave, in a mess of confusion and embarrassment.

'Once that is done,' said Zhou, 'could you possibly return to the Protectorate augmentation and rate it again? You might find it more agreeable. Personally, it's always been one of my favourites. It must have been a wonderful place in which to grow up.'

Fosse thanked him again, and went straight to sickbay. The hazer was the smallest of wafers added to the neck implant. It took no more than a few minutes to add.

After that, Cee's face was no longer so clear in his mind, and neither was the blow of the axe. It was like watching the event happen to someone else. He was now a bystander to his own rage and fear, and although it was still upsetting to behold, it did not threaten his own idea of who he was. He slept better, and stopped checking his hands regularly for signs of the infection, whatever it had been. It had not touched him, after all.

THE IDEA THAT he was labelled within some system that he could not access bothered him less as time passed. It became easier to believe there was some secret part of him, deep inside, that remained untouched by everything: the Protectorate, the past, even the present that he lived through without care. Months went by.

'Fosse Davey.'

Was time repeating itself? Li Zhou, in the same suit, wearing the same expression, standing in the doorway while Fosse worked out. But this time the gym was a red pillared hall of floating dragons, teeth bared, eyes wild, each one waiting to be conquered, and Fosse closed the augmentation down with reluctance. He'd been allocated a triple shift at the last minute, covering for an illness, and was making the most of his free time, before the hard work began.

'I thought I might try exercising more,' said Zhou.

'Really?' said Fosse.

'I thought you might help me get started.'

'Coach will—'

Zhou gave a very small smile, and shook his head. Of course, he knew all about what Coach could and couldn't do for him. 'I was hoping for the personal approach,' he said.

'I'm not good at being personal.'

'Forgive me, but I'm not certain that applies to all forms of expression.'

Those blue eyes, accessing all that data. What did the records say? No doubt they included a breakdown of the hours he spent alone, and the fact that he'd opted for the sexual suppressant back on board the ship when the dreams of Victoria and Annie had got too much for him to bear. He felt naked.

'You're not dressed for exercising,' he said.

'No. I can see I should be honest. I have a proposal to put to you, and I wanted to take time to get to it, but maybe if would be better if I simply…'

'Yes,' said Fosse.

'Yes, yes. Your verbal skills are poor, we know that, but you have a very clear connection with Coach. Your senses, your feelings. There's a theory that people who grow up without an implant have less defences against the—anyway. We wondered if you might be interested in another role here. How are you finding Logistics?'

'It's fine.' The truth was that, over time, the repetitive nature of the work had begun to bother him. He'd accessed Coach's suggestion garden and planted a seed asking if work couldn't also be augmented with scenarios, but had found a virtual bunch of azaleas in his room with a card letting him know that such an approach had to be discounted as it might lead to safety issues.

'I can see you're finding it a little frustrating. You enjoy a lot of the augmentations, don't you? Coach is looking into the possibility of offering Qitan scenarios, since physical tourism has been closed down, but they need accurate emotional responses to reality interfacing in order to create them. Nobody has travelled much beyond the base for quite a few years now, since the Geli Accords. How would you like to go? See Qita?'

'I'm not good at—'

'No, I know, but it's all through the implant. We record what you do, what you see, but most importantly, what you feel. Speaking is irrelevant. This is to be an authentic experience, so we need someone physically fit, who can withstand travelling, a bit of hardship in their living conditions. Also the language—the way the brain works, the team feels that multilingualism might be a drawback. Do you see why we're asking you? To be honest, there are so few people who might fit the role.'

'Yes, I can see that,' said Fosse. 'Can I think about it?'

'Of course!' Zhou smiled. 'I see you have a triple shift coming up. Think about it while you're working. That should be ample time.'

So the extra shifts were an unsubtle form of manipulation. A trick. He thought of Cee, waving his hands, saying whatever needed to be said to get the result he wanted. *Fuck all lies and liars*, he thought, and the implant blunted the anger for him, but still, it was there. It would never quite go away.

He could easily have hurt Zhou, at that moment. Even hobbled, his brain curtailed and controlled, he was still scared that he could become a danger; and now he was powerful, muscular. A man. It was the worst thing he could imagine.

To be outside, freed from the base, from people: was he trying to escape again? Could that ever be done?

'Okay,' he said. 'Yes. I'll go.'

'That's great,' said Zhou. 'I really think this is a wonderful opportunity for you.'

Had he really been given a choice at all? It didn't matter. The Coalition wanted him willing, and he was. He would run far away and let them record their results, all over the beauty spots of Qita, as long as he did not have to play any more games, or feel the urge to hurt anyone again.

Later, when he packed for the trip, he took out the axe handle splinter from the desk drawer once more. He wanted it with him, but he couldn't bear the thought of carrying it.

Eventually he put it back in the drawer and left it there.

'No,' said Fosse. 'This way.' He pointed to the rising hills.

'That isn't the right direction,' said the guide. It had turned to face the human-built highway, which had carried only light traffic since movement across Qita had been reduced to a minimum after the Accords. Essential journeys and unmanned freight only. It felt good to have been labelled as *essential*, supplied with documents that proclaimed his importance, but to travel on the highway itself—surely that was too obvious? He was meant to be seeing the real Qita.

'I was told to go anywhere, see anything,' Fosse told the guide, who didn't even appear to be listening. There was very little to the Qitan's behaviour that he recognised—a lack of assumed human characteristics that had made the few dealings he'd had with the locals in the workplace easier. It stood still with its eyes fixed on the road, its large chin wobbling.

'I told your people I have a path to walk,' it said. 'No transport, no cruiser. I say where we go.'

'An agreed path?'

'I told them you are free to come with me. That's all.'

'That's not what I was told.'

'They don't care what they told you,' said the Qitan. 'Why should you care?'

Fosse shifted his backpack. It contained many items, procured somehow for him, from a list he'd made based on his camping experiences with his uncle. A map, a compass, a stove, a pot, a water canteen, and pre-packaged food; and a tent, of course. His uncle had made carrying all these things look easy, but in truth it was a hard, uncomfortable weight on his back. He ached already.

The Qitan didn't appear to have any possessions with it. It wore a bulky orange jumpsuit of some slippery, reflective material. Perhaps the suit held deep pockets.

'But I want to go—' said Fosse, but the guide simply starting walking, and the battle was lost. He had to follow. He would not be in charge after all. In truth, it was a relief. What did he know about this place, anyway? His mother had been here before him, but nothing here reminded him of her, or of Isley, who had been too human in his surfing shirts.

This Qitan was a different kind of being. He watched the easy swing of the Qitan's arms as it walked ahead of him, along the verge of the highway. It had purpose, and that was so much better than anything Fosse had. What difference would the direction make, when all he wanted was to get away from himself?

He fell into the rhythm of walking, and began to leave Tung Base behind. The sounds and sights of the world penetrated his thoughts, drawing him out of his own mind to see clearly the purple mountains and the pink-tinged sky, the plants that waved to their own internal music, the soft warm breeze that permanently stole over his skin. There were no other Qitans nearby, but even if there had been, he would not have felt threatened. They all lived without conflict, in harmony.

He wondered where the road led to. He asked

Coach, and then remembered with the fresh shock of bereavement that Coach's interface had been turned off. It would record his thoughts, but there would be no more instant answers. He was alone again.

At least the block on his sharpest memories remained in place.

He found himself thinking of his mother once more; it was becoming a habit, now he was such a gaping spatial distance from her. It seemed to lessen the gap in other ways. Had she ever left the base? Seen this world as he saw it now? She had never spoken with him of her time commissioned. While she was stationed here, tourism had been allowed; perhaps she had travelled on this very highway. He didn't like the idea. He pushed it aside.

The Qitan had slowed pace to the point where Fosse had to catch up with him or look deliberately rude. As he drew alongside, it said, 'I have been told your mission is to visit places, but I don't know if I believe that.'

'If you don't believe it, why would you help me?'

'You must make your decisions while I make mine. It doesn't matter either way.'

'Well,' Fosse said. 'I am just here to see things.'

'For what purpose?'

'So they can be explained to people back on Earth.'

'You'll explain the things you see?'

'No, a machine will.'

'The machines you put in your head?'

'Yes.' Fosse licked his lips. 'Does that... upset you?'

'No, no. I have wondered if the machine and the human grow together?'

'Machines don't grow,' said Fosse. 'They are not alive. But they can be instructed to explain many things to people when they're told to.'

'That is a lot of explanation for everyone involved,' observed the guide. 'It's odd. That's my favourite word in your language. Odd. It's no good in any other language.'

'How many languages do you speak?'

'All of them.'

'Don't be ridiculous.'

'I'm not.' It stopped walking and waved its arms over its head. What did that mean? It was a bizarre gesture. 'I speak all your languages.'

Fosse asked Coach for an exact number of languages currently spoken on Earth, then, in the absence of an answer, of real information, made up a number instead. 'There are over a thousand languages on Earth.'

'No, there are six. Chinese, Russian, Urdu, Swahili, Spanish, English.'

'That's just the ones on the base,' said Fosse. 'On Earth, there are many more.'

It opened its mouth and poked out its tongue. 'No,'

it said. 'I didn't think your land could be so interesting. Name these languages. Make a list. Speak them.'

'I can't speak them.'

'Speak some.'

'I can't speak any,' said Fosse. 'Except English.'

The guide began walking once more. The tongue was poked out again. Was it a gesture that meant amusement, or surprise? Once he had the suspicion he was being laughed at, he felt free to retaliate. There was to be no polite formality between them. 'How do you speak any Earth languages at all?' he asked, enjoying the pace they kept between them, and the mild breeze on his face.

'I worked on your base for a long time, and I listened. I like to learn. It's odd. Too many meanings squeezed into every word, and all said the same with different letters. What a mess.'

Fosse laughed. 'I can't disagree with that.'

'All languages have their own music, I think.' It opened its mouth and sang, creating harmonising sounds, as if two or three people were singing together.

'What was that?' Fosse asked.

'The name of my language. Qitan, as you call it. Odd word. Odd.'

'Say the name of your planet.'

Another song.

'Wow,' said Fosse. 'I didn't know you could make such

complicated sounds. I don't think anybody at home knows. In my part of the world, anyway.'

'It is private.'

'You don't seem to find it private.'

'I'm very old and badly behaved in company,' said the guide, as if that explained everything, and Fosse was delighted to find that it did.

'Very old and very odd,' he said.

'Yes! Old and odd. I like words that work together. Tell me more.'

So the conversation started, and it didn't stop.

WHY WAS IT so easy to speak to the guide? Fosse had never felt such freedom before. The meanings of words no longer weighed down his mouth before he spoke— what did it matter if he couldn't be accurate, or if he was too precise, and revealed the deepest, worst parts of himself in the process? The guide didn't assume to understand beyond its experiences. It passed no judgement, and seemed to expect a gap to exist between them that communication couldn't bridge.

It never asked for his name, and Fosse did not want to give one, or receive one in return.

*　　*　　*

THE TENDENCY TO ask Coach questions, so quickly established in his mind, transferred itself entirely to the guide. Fosse suspected part of the reason for this was the strangeness of the answers it provided.

'How many Qitans are there on your world?' he said, as they walked the highway.

'Less,' it said. 'I know there are very many more humans, am I right?'

'I don't know.'

'How can you not know?' It seemed genuinely indignant at the idea.

'Okay,' said Fosse. 'There are more.'

'More?' The guide squatted on its haunches and put its palms to the highway—a gesture it often made, to the point that Fosse had begun to suspect it was in some kind of close unspoken communication with the land itself, possibly receiving directions, or instructions.

Hands.

Nothing reminded him more of home. He tried his hardest to not look at his own hands. They were tools, nothing more.

The established rhythms of Tung Base, with its work shifts, began to leave him, and the guide made decisions about when to eat and when to rest. If there was a regular pattern to the stops, Fosse couldn't find it.

The suit the guide wore could be folded out to create a

small triangular tent. Long sticks of chewy food, possibly a processed vegetable, could be produced from slits inside the long arms and legs. The guide never offered to share, and Fosse did not proffer his own dried packets. He felt utterly separate from his travelling companion, and in their distinct identities lay a paradox: never had he felt such shared, mutual purpose before.

When the highway came to an abrupt end, Fosse felt disappointment. The first stage of the journey was over, and all they had found was one of the Coalition's many mining facilities. A set of gates stood across the road, and a running line of high link fence ran in a straight line, beyond his line of sight in either direction.

The place was locked up tight. Nobody was on guard duty, and the cameras on the fences did not complete watchful arcs of movement, unlike the ones at Tung. Squat grey temporary buildings, obviously military, were lined up in a grid, but nobody moved between them. It was eerie.

'Things grow,' said the guide. It pointed at the ground. Fosse followed the line of its finger and saw a fresh peppering of orange plant growth poking up through the ground of the base; it had been empty for some time.

Behind the buildings was a larger structure: a vast white barrel sitting on a tripod. It reached high into the sky; Fosse had to crane his head to see the top of it.

'What is that?' asked the guide.

'I don't know.'

'You don't know, I don't know, you don't know. How can you say you don't know? This is your way of doing things.'

'I don't know how mining works. I'm in Logistics. I carry things. I thought the mines were all operational, but it's so quiet.'

'Everyone is at Tung now. A subtraction. A retraction.' It repeated the words a few times. It enjoyed language in a way that made Fosse envious.

'So where do we go? Left or right?'

'In.'

'We can't get in.'

The guide swung its arms, windmilling. 'Like this,' it said.

'We're going to fly over?'

Its tongue poked out. Yes, it was definitely a sign of amusement. 'Fly. Try to fly. Please. I will watch you.'

'This is ridiculous,' Fosse said, mainly to himself, but also to the place in general. When it came to recreating Qita from his experiences, would the team of computer experts imbue all this with the tinge of unreality he felt? Or was that in his mind alone?

'We will rest now.' The guide began the process of unfolding its suit, revealing the soft bluish skin of its torso. Its limbs were thin, but its stomach area sagged and rippled. Perhaps those folds were the signs of ageing.

'Maybe less, now,' said Fosse, suddenly.

'Less.'

'Less humans. When I left there was a—a disease. Spreading. Illness. I don't know what it was. Quarantine. When you lock things up tight and leave them. Nobody allowed in or out. Do you know that concept?'

'Less is better than more,' it said, setting to work on the construction of its tent. 'It's the end we move towards, when we walk, when we live. Where I am going.'

Was it talking about death? 'No, no, no,' said Fosse, firmly. He didn't want to talk about that.

Its tongue protruded once more. The tent constructed, the guide crawled inside, and was silent.

FOSSE SLEPT DEEPLY, and when he emerged from his own tent, dry-mouthed and fuzzy-headed, he found himself looking at a large square hole in the ground, the cut edges of the ground fresh and oozing. The guide stood next to a matching hole on the other side of the fence.

'Hello,' it said. 'If you find it difficult to fly, then you can maybe…' It windmilled its arms once more.

Fosse approached the hole. It was easily wide enough to admit him. He couldn't tell how far it went down;

after a few feet it was filled with muddy brown water.

'Swim,' said Fosse. 'You want me to swim.'

'Is that your word? Swim.'

'Did you make this hole?'

'I have a tool.'

'You made a tunnel with a tool and now I should swim to you?'

'No! Not now,' said the guide. 'You would leave behind all your many possessions. Pick them up first, and put them in your bag.'

'Backpack.'

'Backpack. Backpack.' Another word it liked. It repeated it over and over as Fosse did as he was told, all the time thinking about the darkness of the hole, about swimming through it, holding his breath, keeping his eyes tightly shut. If the guide could do it, he could do it. Wasn't that true? He wasn't certain it was true.

He put on his loaded backpack and crouched on the edge of the hole.

'Don't drink any,' said the guide. 'Swim down, and then along.'

'I can't do it,' Fosse said. He felt breathless.

'You can't swim?'

'No, I can swim.' He thought of Black Torr Hole, the pond near home. Not home, he corrected; near where he had lived. He had spent days there, diving in and crawling out, enjoying the shock of slipping from the grassy edge into the cold water, the snatching away of his breath. The contraction of his lungs before taking a deep dive, swimming the entire length of it underwater to impress his uncle, who clapped as he surfaced. Picnics. Camping.

He pushed himself from the side of the hole, bracing himself for the cold, but the water was comfortably warm: body temperature. He inhaled, then sank down, keeping his eyes shut as the water closed over his head. The darkness was instant and enclosing. Time slowed, created a space into which fear could spread, but it could only have been a few seconds before his feet touched a smooth, solid surface and he reached forward, felt for his way. There were no barriers before him. He could walk through the tunnel, upright, pushing against the resistance of the water. He could feel whorls of water, small whirlpools, on his face. He had the feeling that if he opened his eyes he would see blackness, yes, but within it, faces he knew well: his mother, down there with him, and Annie and Victoria and Doctor Clarke and so many others, and even Mrs Satterly, and Bailey the dog. He did not open them. He was afraid to see Cee.

He touched a hard surface with his outstretched hands.

Time to surface. He pushed up with his feet and his fear returned; a flash of panic shot through him as his lungs began to strain, but then he was up, breaking through, breathing in the calm, clear air of Qita. He levered himself out of the hole and the water drained from him in streams.

'And now we walk some more. But not for very long,' said the guide, who stood a little distance away, his attention on the giant tripod.

Fosse got to his feet. 'All right,' he said. 'Let's walk.'

THEY PASSED THE squat buildings, and then skirted around the tripod and barrel. It offered no clues as to its purpose, even in close proximity. The orange stubble poking from the ground became longer, tougher. Soon they were wading through it, the blades as strong and sharp as reeds, and when Fosse looked up from the task of negotiating a path he was surprised to find there was only a few feet of plant growth left before they reached a small natural harbour, a very white beach of fine sand, and regularly spaced stone pillars, to which were tied five boats.

'Sailing!' said Fosse. He had very little experience with boats. His uncle had arranged for them both to go fishing with one of the local crews—*life experience*, his uncle had called it, and there had been so many striped mackerel pulled on board by thin, dangling strings.

They lay shining in the bottom of the boat: stinking rich treasure. His uncle had brought home a share of the catch at the end of the day, and prepared mackerel a different way all week, deciding after an experiment with mackerel omelette that people could certainly eat too much of the stuff. They'd never gone out fishing again.

It was a happy memory. He'd almost forgotten it; it was difficult to drag up past the block in his brain. He wanted to relive it, to feel that way again, but it sank back down and was replaced by another memory: the last time he'd been on board a boat, taking him from the Protectorate to Swansea. The three men and the woman had not even looked at him as he crouched among the ropes and tarpaulins, terrified, certain they would simply throw him overboard rather than take him all the way to his destination. The fear was blunted now. He was glad of the block once more.

'We will take one,' said the guide.

'A boat?' They were about the size of the fishing vessels from home, but sleek and teardrop shaped, dark blue. He approached the closest one. There was no cabin, or visible motor. It did not float in the sea but sat high on it, unmoving. The stillness of it was unnerving. The water churned around it, creating a froth.

'Is this a Qitan boat?' he asked.

'No,' said the guide. 'Let's get on it. We have quite far to go.' It waded out past the pillar and pulled on the taut length of rope attached to the boat, using it to swing on deck. The boat did not move throughout.

'It's not water at all,' said Fosse. He felt stupid to have not realised it earlier. He had heard, had been told in briefing, that the main trade with the Qitans was mining for minerals that were plentiful on this planet but exhausted at home. Was that really the case? He wished he had spent more time asking Coach pertinent questions rather than getting lost within its amusements.

The guide had used some sort of small tool to create a tunnel, but after only a few metres of digging down there had been only this liquid—the same liquid that covered most of the planet. The tripod, and the vast barrel, played on his mind as he followed suit, boarding the craft. There were things he didn't understand, and so many lies.

'I don't get it,' said Fosse. But he sat quietly behind the guide, who put its hands through two circular holes in the bottom of the boat—holes that did not admit any liquid at all—and somehow steered them out to sea, to the tune of a regular beat that rose from the craft itself as it travelled. A steady pulse, like the banging of a hand on a door, demanding admittance, over and over.

*   *   *

IT'S LOVE, THIS is love, what I always imagined love to be: to be inside another, to know them and feel what they feel. It's what I've wanted since the beginning and part of me thought it was an impossible demand. But Isley has given me that gift with his touch.

I was with my son and I understood him, all of him. The part that ever doubted love is shrivelling up, and I'll be glad to see it die.

How is this even possible?

I'm still in the cellar. Fosse is very far away, in time and space. His Qita, the one that awaits him, is so different from the one I knew. But now I see I had changed it to suit my stories every time I drank brew and talked of it. And Fosse will make his own Qita too.

Is it real? I would dismiss it all, this vision, as yet another story, except for the feelings I have. This love. This truth.

'People are here,' says Won.

The sound of her voice brings me fully back to the cellar. My breath is a cloud around me, and my lips and cheeks tingle, but the biting cold does not penetrate me. I am part of Isley now.

Our hands have joined. He is asleep, peaceful. Won's head is still on his neck and chest, her cheek melting into him. She is looking at me. We are becoming something.

What are we becoming?

The banging sounds again. So it was not, is not, only in Fosse's memory.

'It's not over yet,' she says.

'Fosse is on Qita,' I whisper. I need to say it, out loud, to try to make sense of the impossible. 'He's a man.'

'Yes.'

'He's...' He's so many things. My son. I did not know him at all. He's good and bad and all things, my baby, the man. 'But it can't have happened yet. He can't even be on Qita yet, can he? He only left here a few days ago. He might be on board a Coalition ship, leaving today. Right now. I could stop him.'

'How?' says Won. She's so passive, so calm. Like a true Qitan. She thinks it would be useless to break free and journey to my son, to stop this version coming true. Is the future set in stone, like the past, as solid as the fossils of Toulu? She repeats, 'People are here. You need to open the door and let them in.'

More banging. It's low, rhythmic. The heartbeat of the Skyward, I think, has always been the banging on the door for admittance. Everybody has always wanted in.

'Go open up.'

'I can't,' I say, but I have no idea if that's true.

'Don't worry. You can come back.'

I let go of Isley's hand and our skin sticks, then separates into strands that yearn to stay joined. They stretch apart like elastic—no, like the tendrils of a plant that clings to the rockface, finding a crevasse from where life can be drawn. There's no pain. The flesh under my skin is visible. It's soft, jelly-like. It would be so easy to let it have its way and sink back into them entirely, but not yet. I need to know what comes next. I need to open the door.

I pull away until the strands snap, and hang loosely from my hand. I cover them with the sleeve of my jumper and take the stairs up to the bar.

It's daytime. Bright winter sunshine is streaming through the windows. The smell of stale brew and cigarette ash are so strong, and welcome in their familiarity. Things are the same. It brings me back to myself. I can even manage a smile as I unbolt the door and swing it back.

Doctor Clarke looks tired, worn down. He holds a brown leather bag and is wearing a long trench coat, and wellington boots that are thickly splattered with mud. 'I've walked miles,' he says. 'I couldn't get my petrol allowance. They've closed us off completely. Wouldn't even let me near the fence they've put up. I don't think it's Protectorate people. Is Dominic here? I need him to speak to them.'

'He's not.' I let the doctor in. He stands amid the detritus of the bar and frowns as he looks around.

'When's the last time you saw him?'

Years ago. No, that's Fosse's reality, Fosse's memories. My son, the man, is still in my head with all his doubts and withdrawals from the world, his anger and his fear and the things he let into his head to try to make it all go away. I'm full to bursting with it; I could cry out for him, but instead I hear myself asking, 'What day is it? Today?'

'What?'

I repeat the question, slowly, using the words to ground me.

'It's the fifth of November,' says Doctor Clarke. 'Bonfire night.'

I've lost two days, which means I haven't seen Dom in—'A week. It's a week since I've seen Dom. I think.' Where the hell is he? I need him. His energy, his certainty. Maybe he's chasing after Fosse. Yes, that sounds like him. He could be on his way to Swansea right now. Everything can be changed. 'I told Benny Sykes he and Fosse were missing. He said he'd look into it.'

'Fosse is gone as well?'

'Benny said maybe they were camping.'

I can see from Doctor Clarke's face that he doesn't believe it either. 'Are you all right?' He glances at my hands, at the sleeve pulled low. 'Are you showing symptoms?'

'No, this is—'

'Jemima,' he says. 'Show me your hand.'

He's been my doctor since I was a child. I have an automatic response to that tone: I hold out my hand.

He looks at loose shreds of skin, slowly knitting themselves back together. He doesn't attempt to touch them. 'You have it,' he says. 'It's spreading through the region. But it's not bad in your case, Jem. I've seen much worse. Listen, I need to set up a treatment centre—I think this would be the best location. Everybody knows it, and its high up, overlooking the village. I went to the Schilling Barn first and that's—the ground is, well, it's not solid, it's the same in lots of places that are lower down now and there are animals trapped. I've seen *people* trapped, but I...' He stops himself, shakes his head.

My hand is red and alive, and the skin moves by itself. 'This is the disease?' I ask him.

'It's the reason for the quarantine. They're calling it a disease, but I don't know what it is. It's not a virus. It's only affecting your hand now, so you have time. It might not spread any further. Can you help? Set the Skyward up as a centre? We'll get through this together.'

I want to laugh. Together, apart: these words are losing their meaning to me. Nothing is separate. Everything, together. 'Yes, of course,' I tell him. 'We should be together. Together.'

He slumps in relief. He is tired, and fighting hard against the thing he doesn't understand, even though it's not his kind of problem at all. He's so human. 'I'll make some posters, put them up around the area. Can you welcome anyone who turns up before I get back? Make them comfortable?'

'Everyone's welcome here. I'll leave the door open from now on.'

'Right. I'll be back as soon as I can.'

I look at his hands. The palm of his left hand is wrapped in a neat bandage. He sees me notice it. He sighs, a long breath out, and then begins to talk. It's a low escape of pressure from inside him, and it's a prayer.

'I could say something about bringing you into this world, Jem, but to be honest I don't remember it, exactly. After you or your brother was born, I have a memory of that. I'm not sure which one of you it was. It was early morning.'

'That would have been Dom, then.' I was born in the evening, at teatime, or so the story goes.

He nods. 'Early morning, leaving your parents' house with the view down over the estate to the church: I can picture it. I walked back through the village. It was very quiet, except for the bakery; fresh bread was already being baked, of course. Whenever I smell it now, I think of that morning. I don't know how to describe it except to say that everything seemed to be just as it should be. The lawns, the gardens. The mown grass of the green, the smoke from the chimneys, and a new baby born. What a blessing. I'd come from the city, moved here in my twenties, and never regretted it. It was everything I'd never had: the fresh air, the coast, the trees, and the solid brick houses. You know, I think I've remembered that moment for all these years because it was the first time I felt properly included. Part of this place. Then I couldn't stand the thought of a world without our village in it, like villages used to be, should be. But here we are. Today.

'I look over the moors and I don't recognise them, Jem. I fought so hard for it all. I can't let it end.'

I watch him go, walk away over the moors. He may claim not to recognise the path, but he walks it in the same way he always has, towards the village, filled with his own purpose.

He spoke as if we shared a vision of this land on which we live. I should have told him that his version of the village was never real to anybody but him.

I leave the door wide open, as promised, and return to the cellar.

Back down in the darkness, Isley is still asleep.

'He's lost in Qita,' says Won, fondly. 'He missed it so, even though he didn't want to be part of it, in the end.' She has put a hand on his chest since I went upstairs and it has fixed in place, grown into him. I feel a sudden reflex of disgust, wrongness. This disease is moving fast, and I'm so scared of it. But love, the memory of that love, and my son. I have to be a part of it again. Is that future set? I don't know. I think of Dom being born: the promise of the new baby at sunrise.

'Do you know where Dom is?' I ask her. 'My brother. You met him, back when you first arrived.' That feels like a very long time ago. Another theory occurs to me: Dom's gone to get help. He's crossed the border, used his politician's tricks to find medical assistance for us all. He's persuading everyone to be a better version of themselves; that's what he does. I've never realised before how much faith I have in his ability to fix things. No—not fix things. In his ability to be himself, and for that purity of purpose to work on others.

Won doesn't answer me. 'I never wanted this to happen,' she says. 'When I first landed here, I was terrified in case it did. We tried so hard to keep separate, all of us. But now it's happening, it's a good thing. I wonder what we were all so scared of.'

'More people are coming here,' I tell her. 'They've got hands like mine. They've got this disease, whatever it is.'

'There'll be space,' she says, then, 'I'm very hungry.'

'I could find you something.'

'No, thank you. I'll be fine.'

'A cup of mint tea, then?'

'No. No, it's fine.'

The incongruity of offering a cup of tea to a body who's stuck to another body who I happen to also want to get stuck to—yes, it hits me, hard, and I laugh, and I can't stop, and she watches me, and Isley wakes up and says, 'What's so funny?' But before I can even begin to explain it, he reaches his hand out to me and I take it, and sit by his side, and everything is perfect. How much easier this is if I don't think about it. We're all laughing together, together, many ways, in many worlds.

THE GUIDE HAD, during its time on the base, learned to laugh like a human. It liked to laugh a lot.

Fosse often found himself laughing along. They set each other off, one laughing, the other joining in. They laughed loudly and freely at everything. At jokes that weren't there and the big joke of the journey they undertook.

He had caught himself performing Qitan actions too. He had a feeling they weren't polite ones. He let his tongue loll out after a particularly good laughing session, and he had the strong sense that it was not an act of imitation on his part. It felt satisfying, deep down. They were coming together, taking parts of each other and making them mutual. These new similarities were a shared symptom of how their lives were aligning.

FOSSE HAD NO idea how much time had passed. A lot, he guessed. There was no discernible structure to time on Qita that he could find. The one sun shone endlessly; a light breeze blew. The climate did not change. They had sailed across open liquid for a time. When the guide had removed its hands from the holes in the craft, they had been stripped of skin, raw and glistening, reminding him of some of his worst memories. But it had read his expression and reassured him: *it does not hurt*, it had said. *It's not a bad thing*. After a time of walking, sleeping, eating, walking, sleeping, eating, the skin had grown back.

They traversed a long plain on which only one crop grew. It looked a little like wheat, but moved in its own time around them. 'Who planted it?' he asked, but the guide did not seem to understand the concept. It stroked the plant as they walked.

'Doesn't that feel strange?' Fosse asked. 'On your new skin?'

'It feels pleasant. We are close. Not far to go.' The guide stopped walking and pulled a stick of food from the leg of its suit. It took a bite and chewed. Fosse came to a halt too and looked around. He hadn't been taking in the surroundings for some time. It was beautiful, but beauty had a way of becoming commonplace when it remained the same, neither shrinking nor stretching; it simply was a snug fit, enclosing him, keeping him comfortable. Where was he? He had no clue. He hadn't even thought to ask; he'd become used to simply following.

Ahead, mountains rose.

'Is that the same mountain range that's next to Tung Base?'

'No,' said the guide. 'Did you think I had led you around in a circle?'

'No, I just…'

'We have walked across Shanlingu.'

'Shanlingu?' He knew the story. The two armies had met, and not a single death had resulted. The Qitans had agreed to let humanity explore their planet in peace and harmony. He remembered it from a geography lesson.

'The beginning of the white path,' said the guide. It said something—a repeated cadence—in its own language and lifted up its hands to the sky. A gesture of joy. Fosse wondered how it had ever seemed unclear to him.

'A holy place,' said Fosse. Of course. A culture that believed in peace would worship at a site where bloodshed was avoided. It made sense.

'I don't know what that means,' it said to him. 'Do you see the stick? Ahead? We are going there.'

'Where?' Fosse squinted into the distance, where the plain met the first rise of the mountain. He could see nothing of interest.

'Come.'

They walked on.

'IT HAS BEEN a rare time of peace,' said the guide, later. 'It has been very calm. Not like when I was young. Not at all. We have humans to thank for many things.'

'You weren't peaceful before we turned up?'

'No,' it said. 'Some of the young Qitans did not want to become old Qitans. Were you peaceful—humans, I mean—peaceful before you could come to Qita?'

'We've never been peaceful,' Fosse told him.

'Then you have to thank us too.'

Fosse had found a weird kind of relief in many of the guide's stranger statements, but not this time. There was something else going on here—something he wanted to pin down. He tried to keep irritation from his voice as he said, 'You fought each other? Young against old?'

The guide's tongue emerged, lolled from its mouth as it walked. The act gave the impression that it was deep in thought, but in an unguarded, possibly obscene way, like an old man who had forgotten to do up his trousers after a visit to the bathroom, so lost was he in thoughts.

'These terms do not matter now, but I was born on one side of what you call the Nanbu Queeling. We were a large family, there were very many of us created at the same time. An old family. The family on the other side was from a new time. Do you understand? I would not talk of such things, but we are near the end, so I am not so concerned about scaring you.'

'Why would I be scared?' asked Fosse.

The guide went on, 'There are always many reasons to argue and many of them were very important, back then, before. I killed many Qitans. I was...' It searched for a word, then said, 'an engineer. I made a weapon that could dig down, then send up fire, underneath them. This was before the end. It was the will of the...' It said a word in its own language again. 'There is no translation.'

'Elders? Leaders? The Qitans who were in charge?'

'Oh, no,' said the guide. 'Qitans aren't in charge. Not now.'

Then who was? So many things that Fosse had assumed were static on this planet were simply not fixed. Qitan society had changed since the arrival of the Coalition. And everybody had assumed that they were looking at, taking part in, a long-established way of being. Frozen in time and space. But the more Fosse thought about it, the more obvious it became. Humans had been through so many changes. Evolutionary changes, yes, but more than that, much more than that. Who lived where and who loved what and who hated who: what was allowed and what was forbidden, and all of it changing, changing with every generation. Coming from the Protectorate— the place that had redefined itself in the space of a few short years to reject so much—he should have seen it from the beginning.

Earth was far from perfect, and Qita was far from perfect. Nobody was perfect, not from the beginning. There wasn't a place in the universe that was unchangeably perfect.

They were like him. Everyone was like him.

He stopped walking. He put his hands up to the sky, and expressed joy.

'Because we killed each other?' said the guide.

'Yes,' said Fosse. 'Because of that.'

A POLE WAS stuck fast in the ground.

'It's human,' said Fosse. 'It's military.'

'Yes. It's where the white path begins.'

'But it can't have been here long. I thought this was an established path. A trail.'

In the distance, part of the way up the mountain, two figures were visible, holding hands. Qitans. The guide waved at them, and they lifted their joined hands, then turned and walked away, behind a rise of rocks. 'See?' it said. 'It is a known path. Others are taking it.'

'No, I meant—'

'You can read the message. That will help.'

There was a piece of paper attached to the top of the pole. Fosse stepped forward and flipped it over. The paper was neatly divided into sections. Chinese lettering filled one, down one side of the page. The others were Russian, Urdu, Swahili, Spanish, and markings that Fosse assumed were Qitan in origin, although he'd never seen a written version of their language before. The bottom section, smaller than the others, contained a message written in English.

WE OFFER THE HAND OF FRIENDSHIP TO
JOIN OUR GREAT NATIONS.
WE BRING PEACE AND OPPORTUNITIES
FOR A BRIGHTER FUTURE,
AND WE WISH TO SHARE OUR
KNOWLEDGE AND RESOURCES.

'A message of peace,' he said. It felt standard to him, perfunctory. He could imagine many thousands of these things being dropped over vast distances, sent all over the planet. Disposable sentiments for a conquering nation.

'Are there many of these messages?' he asked.

'In this part of Qita, I know of a few. They make up the white path. But I come from here! I wouldn't know of other places.'

'You don't communicate with Qitans in other countries?'

The guide said, 'Let's sit.' Once they were both settled, it began a long explanation with a patient air that could have been entirely imagined, on Fosse's part. It spoke of the planet not as a whole, but as many, many parts. It spoke of places where the weather was too rough to bear, where only the smallest burrowing creatures could live, and of places too hot or too cold for Qitans. Some of the creatures were without intelligence and some were clever. Some crawled, some walked, some flew, some swam. Some lived on islands and some in mountains. *So many, but not anymore here. Just Qitans here, living in...*

'In friendship,' said Fosse, slowly.

'That's right. In friendship. We choose friendship, at the end. Now. Those who do not choose it go elsewhere.'

'I didn't know any of this.' He wondered how many people—humans—did know it. The planet offered huge diversity, and Qitans were a tiny part of that.

'You are very young,' observed the guide. 'Perhaps they did not want to scare you either. Also, the young can be difficult. Sometimes they think separation is better. We have that on Qita, too. They think they'll find answers that are special. They're not like those that came before, are they?' It stuck out its tongue.

Divisions between generations: another thing they had in common.

'Can you draw it for me? Qita?'

The guide began to trace symbols on the ground, radiating out from the pole. It drew with speed and confidence, and where it touched, liquid welled up from the earth to fill the grooves. The liquid was silvery blue in places, and greener in others. It was impossible to tell what the colours meant.

It was a map.

The map grew and grew. So many marks. Fosse stood back as the guide worked, moving outwards in a spiral, counter-clockwise from the pole. The planet was a swirl that it created. It reminded Fosse of the whirlpools that he had seen forming on the side of the boat, and felt on his face as he walked the length of the tunnel. It grew larger and larger. At times the marks reminded him of mathematical symbols, or of Kanji, or English letters, but they never made sense. Shapes, too. A triangle, at times. A simple drawing of a cat, or maybe a house?

He wanted to find meaning where none could exist, for him, except in the broadest sense—this was Qita. When the guide drew a circle around the whole, enclosing all the marks and stepping back from its work, Fosse knew it for sure. Qita, a whole: complex and diverse and so much more than he had ever been told, ever expected. His mission was to explore Qita, and he now knew that was an impossibility. It was as terrifying and magnificent and unknowable as Earth. The smallest part around Tung Base was all he could ever hope to visit.

He wished he could record the guide's drawing, to keep forever. Then he remembered Coach, in his head, and was glad. This would not be lost. Coach could keep it, perfectly, and show it to the whole of Earth, enhancing everyone's understanding of this planet. He knew he was being ridiculously optimistic, but he had to believe it. It was too painful to think this moment, this drawing, would mean nothing.

'Hm,' said the guide, then made harmonic sounds in its own language. 'We'll go further on the white path, and you'll understand better. Let's go forward.'

The liquid drained back into the ground and the marks faded. Only the pole and the leaflet were left.

*   *   *

How DO YOU *tell someone that the thing they think is special is nothing but humanity being its usual self?* Fosse wondered, as they journeyed over the mountains. The leaflet had created a path, a journey solemnly undertaken, and it was nothing but a piece of propaganda.

He thought about it a lot, as time passed. He was certain the same was true from the Qitans' perspective, too; whatever encapsulated normality for them could only be amazing and strange to humanity. But surely there were moments, small individual happenings, where they could meet on neutral terms and understand each other properly and fully. Wasn't that what he was doing with the guide? Or was he overestimating his own importance? He began to hate being human, particularly when the soft downy hair on his upper lip and chin turned hard and itchy, and began to form a beard. He pulled on it as it grew longer, and wished it would go away. It reminded him he was part of that other planet, Earth, no matter where he travelled.

He was learning, and ageing.

Am I a man now? he asked himself. He was no longer sure that it was a level that could be achieved: a plateau, a stopping point with a view over all that had gone before.

We offer the hand of friendship: the leaflet had said. The kind of friendship in which one side took everything they wanted, and the other side let them in the name of the promise given. He had experience of that. But his worst memories continued to fade, as did his best. Earth was very far away.

Fosse asked questions often as the journey stretched onwards and upwards to a high, clear peak that revealed endless seas ahead, all around, apart from a spit of land that widened into a settlement. The guide suggested they camp at the highest peak, looking down over the view, and then they started back down the other side of the mountain. Once, the guide had killed his own kind over such delineations as which side of the hill he lived, and who was older or younger. It seemed both ridiculous and utterly believable, and there was nothing to show for it.

Fosse felt changed; changed again.

He ran out of supplies and switched to Qitan food and drink, which the guide was happy to supply; it showed no signs of running low. The sticks were spicy, and the drink was warming, pleasant. Still he continued to ask questions, but he could not shape them to fit into the lock of the guide's knowledge, and eventually he gave up trying. They played word games instead. Words that sounded the same and meant different things. Two and too. Seen and scene. Not and knot.

*　　*　　*

'THIS IS NOT a knot,' says Isley. 'It's not a knot.'

I don't want to open my eyes. I want to stay on Qita, with Fosse, inside Isley, floating in both homes. I was becoming and belonging. Everything is there to be known.

'It's not a knot. Not yet,' he says, and pushes me away. Our hands break apart and I fall to the floor. The connection is broken, and it hurts, it hurts to be back in the Skyward, and the cellar is very cold and very damp. I can hear water running, somewhere close. I feel empty, thirsty. I want a drink. Human concerns. I could happily leave them all behind. Is that what's happening to me? Am I leaving humanity behind?

'Jem?'

A woman's voice, familiar, coming from upstairs. Calling for me. It's my name. I remember, yes, it's my name.

'You'd better go,' says Isley. 'But come back soon, okay? Come back soon.' He smiles at me. He's in a playful mood; I can't remember seeing him like this before. As if a weight has been lifted from him. I feel I know him so much better, but not in the usual way, as one face talking to another. From the inside out.

It's too much, it's overwhelming. It makes no sense, and I can't understand why that doesn't bother me more. But I can't give it up now. I reach for him again—

'Jem? Dom?' calls the voice.

'Go on,' he tells me, and I make my way upstairs.

A person is standing in the bar. It's night, and the moonlight through the open doorway is not enough to help me identify them; it's the dog that does, the patient sturdy dog standing by their side who could only be Bailey.

'Hi Freya,' I say.

'I had to come,' Freya says. 'My house is underwater. It's flooded. The village is flooded.' She says this with wonder, pleasure. Freya, who lived for decades in that house, giving herself to the community to protect this idea of perfect rural life. Is it so easy to give up on this way of life? Surely she should mourn it. But then I remember that her husband is dead, and I think I can understand why she has decided to mourn no longer.

Bailey is wearing socks on his paws, held up with string. He looks clownish, and also wise, and very pleased to see me, in that way only dogs can manage. He wags his tail, and I go to him, and stroke his head.

'I saw Doctor Clarke's message,' Freya goes on, 'It said to come here, but I knew that anyway. Bailey knew it too. Where's Dom?'

My brother really is the hub of this village. I hatch a new theory: whatever this disease is, he'll be at the centre of it, battling it from the inside out. Dealing with it. 'He's not here. Fosse is gone too.'

She nods, as if that makes sense, or possibly she's not really listening to me. There are things she wants to do and say. 'Am I the first?'

'The first for the treatment centre? I haven't really—there's not a space that—'

'Come on, Bailey.' She pushes past me, and Bailey follows, through the bar, into the hall. She glances up the stairs, then turns to the cellar. 'Down, I'm guessing.'

'No, Freya, there's nothing...' I don't want her to go down there. But this feeling, this feeling that the future is no different to the past and neither of them can be altered, is taking me over; no matter how we tell it, how the limbs grow or are amputated, how the mouths move or the eyes see, the spirit remains the same. Is that the right word for it? Spirit? I find myself wanting to believe that something inside remains intact.

'I don't want to be alone,' she says, at the top of the stairs. She's waiting for something. For me. 'But I'm scared, Jem. I have to admit I'm a little bit scared.'

'I don't know how to describe what's down there,' I tell her. It's as honest as I can be. 'I don't know if it's good or bad. I don't think those definitions apply.'

'Maybe we'll be better off without all that,' she tells me, surprising me. I've underestimated her. I've been thinking of her as a little old lady, trapped in the thoughts of the generation before my own, but now I catch a glimpse of strength and flexibility. Such a rare combination. I wish I'd known her better, all this time.

On impulse, I put my arms around her and hug her. She hugs me back, tightly. I'm a true human being in this transaction. I have no idea of what she is really thinking, but I try to express my warmth and respect, and I hope she feels it through my skin, somehow.

Then I lead the way down to the cellar.

Won and Isley are playing a game. She puts an ankle to his. Where their bare skin meets, it fuses. Then she pulls her foot back and the skin holds, creating a tunnel that joins them, a fragile, membranous circle, that then breaks apart. A few drops of fluid fall; it has already created a small puddle on the floor. They are both smiling. I wonder if I should feel jealousy, or horror, but emotions like that aren't coming easily to me. I'm calm. I feel far away, with my son. Only a very small voice is saying, over and over: *What's happening to me? What's happening?*

'Hello,' says Freya, warmly, her best smile in place. 'I don't think we've met properly before. I wasn't really a pub person. Tom came sometimes, with Bailey.'

'Yes,' says Isley. 'Tom. I knew him. I was so sorry to hear of your loss. And Bailey, yes, I know Bailey. Hello, Bailey. You can take his socks off now. Although they are very smart.'

'He looks handsome,' says Won.

'They did the trick,' Freya says. 'I don't think he would have walked all the way here otherwise. It was Dom's idea, you know.' She kneels down and unties the strings, and the socks slump down. Bailey lifts each paw in turn, patiently. 'I put my hands in the mud and it said to come here. Mud, speaking to me in my head. They had a word for that when I was young: *touched*, they would have said. But here I am, and I'll be touched if that is what's next, because I felt certain it was Tom's voice. Can you tell me—was it Tom's voice? I suppose it couldn't have been.'

'Has the liquid risen far?' says Won.

'Oh, yes.'

'It won't be long, then,' Won murmurs, to Isley, and he nods. They are so calm. Perhaps they know where this all ends.

'You don't mind?' he asks Freya.

'Why should I mind? This way I get to be with Tom again, don't I?'

'Not exactly,' says Won. 'It's more that nobody will think they're with anybody except everybody.'

'Keep the mumbo-jumbo,' says Freya, and a little part of me cheers for her. We're still human. We're not quite done yet. She straightens up, balls the socks, and puts them in the pockets of her coat. 'Us Devon folk don't really care for that.'

'I thought this was the Protectorate,' says Isley.

'It's always been Devon to me. You can't teach an old dog new tricks.'

'But you can!' says Won, and holds out her free hand to Bailey, who trots over willingly and puts his nose to her stomach. He allows her to tousle his ears. Freya comes to them and does the same, kneeling down to put her head beside him, on Won's lap. Won strokes the grey hair at her crown, too.

I've been so quiet, in the corner of the cellar, watching this choice, trying to understand. It's terrifying to watch it happening. How can she give up her separation, her humanity, to become part of this thing, this mess, this collection of existence? Isn't it better to fight?

I think of Doctor Clarke, and his commitment to resistance. He believed in the village above all else. I can't live that way either.

Isley catches my eye, and he smiles.

'Come back to me,' he says.

We love each other. We have, for the longest time. I'm not sure it matters now. But I feel the power of those years in which we were part of nothing but this inn, because we could not bear to belong anywhere else. Do they count for nothing, now?

'There's everyone and everything inside me, but nobody else fits here but you,' he says, holding out his hand, beckoning to the space where I'm to stay. I could still say no. He's promised me that.

Dom. I call to him, in my mind. *Dom, where are you now?*

I take my spot. We will be captured, held in place. I think of Toulu, and the creatures in the rock. Is that our destiny?

'TOULU,' SAID THE guide.

It wasn't a word Fosse had come across before.

The rock was huge, in the centre of the still lake. It was split in two as if struck by lightning, the sides around the injury scorched, and inside were many patterns, fossils: small shelled creatures held in a frozen moment forever more.

'Are these your ancestors?' Fosse asked.

'What does that mean? They are not part of us. They did not want to become us.'

A form of life that died out, then. Evolution was not a straight line on Qita after all.

The white leaflet was not attached to the rock itself, but to a nearby tree. It was the same as the one at Shanlingu: a generic, multi-language message designed to keep the peace.

'Is this still the white path?' he asked. 'We're following

a trail of Coalition leaflets? I thought it was something historical.'

'Do you mean old?' asked the guide. It had rolled up the legs of its suit to its knees, and was paddling in the lake next to the rock. 'Like me? Rude in polite company?'

'Made up of years of happening,' said Fosse. He felt quite pleased with his definition.

'Toulu is that,' it agreed. 'Things that were before. We can sleep here.'

'No,' Fosse said. He didn't like the place. The fossils, the traces of creatures who had died in some surprise attack—from nature itself, perhaps—unsettled him. The rock cast a long shadow, and when he stood in the darkness, beneath it, he could almost touch a difficult memory, down in the damp, of people, crouching, waiting. He had been very young, he suspected. He had been one among many. It summoned the same feelings of disgust, danger. 'Let's move on.'

'Yes, we can move on. We can travel fast from here, be in town soon.'

A town. Many Qitans, gathered. So far, Fosse had only seen a few figures at a distance, soon disappearing from view again. He'd had the feeling they were avoiding him. But he wanted to be among them in a meaningful way, to record what life was like for them faithfully, realistically, to be conveyed back to Earth. And he wanted the guide to take him, and explain it to him in its own inimitable way.

'Good,' he said. 'How?'

THE ANSWER WAS a canyon, the entrance no wider than their shoulders, almost hidden under an ivy-like growth. They pushed past the leaves and entered the shaded walkway, and immediately Fosse missed the sun. The darkness was not absolute, but he found himself struggling to see far; his eyes had become accustomed to permanent light, even when sleeping. Now he felt vulnerable, weakened. He remembered how he once used to like the night. It was strange how any change could be accepted. No doubt he would adjust to this, too.

A stream cut along the bottom of the canyon, and spongy life sprang up in it. Slippery stuff. It reminded him of seaweed. He concentrated on placing his feet, his Coalition boots proving to be waterproof, and put his hands on the smooth high walls to help him keep his balance. When he looked up, the sky was only a thin strip of light, high above.

It was impossible to talk. Occasionally the guide—permanently ahead of him, as there was no room to walk side by side—would mutter something that Fosse didn't catch. At first he said, 'What?' but the guide never elaborated, and he soon stopped asking.

Old feelings started to return to him—weights that he hadn't really understood he had carried for years: the surety that he was in the wrong place, that he didn't belong, and a particular and bone-deep loneliness. How could those feelings have found him here, so far from Earth and from the boy he had been? He began to feel afraid of more than the dark. He feared regression: returning to what he once was. With fear came anger, and that terrified him too. These emotions fed off each other, got bigger, and it seemed inevitable that they would erupt in violence. He would hurt the guide. He dreaded it, and resented the broad back ahead of him as time passed and the canyon stretched on.

It came to him that the devices implanted within him by the Coalition could no longer be working properly, and as soon as he'd had that thought he lost all confidence in their ability to keep the worst memories away. They poured back in, along with guilt. He talked to himself, blamed himself, begged Cee and Annie and Victoria for forgiveness. And his uncle, and his mother, and everyone he had simply abandoned. It must have hurt them all deeply. He practised conversations in which he asked for their forgiveness, and when he found no replies or answers inside himself, he began to shout. The guide did not turn around, no matter how much noise he made.

He pictured holding the axe again.

He wanted it, to feel safe and strong.

He imagined swinging it once more, connecting with tree, with body, with the guide. He was so scared.

Then his thoughts turned to the graveyard back home. Perhaps it was due to the gloom in the canyon. The graveyard, at night: he had interpreted his visits there as horrific—of course he had, it had been around Halloween, when all such places and adventures are meant to be terrifying—but now, looking back at it, there had been something beautiful about the mud swirling and the body of Tom, so close under the ground, changing, breaking down to feed the trees above. The dog too, Bailey, waiting for him, trusting him: he had loved that dog. He understood, in a burst of laughter, that he still did. Distance did not alter love.

The canyon widened.

The way ahead began to lighten, his thoughts lightening with it. The canyon was releasing its hold upon him. He would emerge from it.

Footsteps in the stream, onwards, onwards, and then a sudden new space, surrounded by people and colour, Qitans, moving and talking and calling in their own tongues. The wide street was made of crushed white rock, still pebbly underfoot, and tall straight houses were arranged in terraced rows.

The change was so abrupt that Fosse turned and looked back at the canyon, wondering if it had simply disappeared. But no, there it was, a dark passage set in a wall, and the wall had been decorated in bold paint—reds and blues and golds—creating a swirling effect.

When he turned back to the town, overwhelmed, speechless, he found the guide facing him with its arms raised. It dropped them and said, 'You suffered. I'm sorry. But it's over now. We've arrived.'

IT LED HIM through the streets.

Many of the houses had open ground floors, pillared, with archways, where Qitans sat and exchanged words or goods. Fosse watched these transactions take place, absorbed in the peaceful way such trades were made. They turned a corner and the shock was instantaneous; they stood before a vast building; crumbling walls that looked much older than everything else nearby. It reminded him of an ancient castle on Earth, and he half-expected to find a portcullis blocking the way. But no, there was only an open gateway, another arch, and then they stood in a square with Qitans walking clockwise, in procession, around the walls, and others gathered under a shady copse of trees in the centre.

'We deserve a drink,' said the guide. 'This is the best

place in town.' It was such a human thing to have said that Fosse laughed.

'You're feeling better. Good.' The guide led him to the trees and settled itself on one of the benches. 'Now we sit and wait.' It patted the space next to it. Self-consciously, Fosse parked himself.

'Who speaks English?' said the guide, loudly, suddenly, and the Qitan at the bench next to them said something in Russian, then something longer in Chinese.

'No, no, no,' said the guide. The Qitan got up and moved to a bench further away.

'Is this... table service?' Fosse asked. 'Shouldn't we be polite?'

'I do not have time for polite,' it told him. 'My feet hurt. I need a drink.' It called out again, in its own language. One of the Qitans walking clockwise around the walls broke from its pattern and came to them.

'I have some English,' it said. 'Used to be humans here often. I learned all their languages. Then they stopped coming. They said they would make the walls better. The walls are coming down. They liked the walls, and said they wanted to save them. They called them... Langzin.'

'They're changeable,' said the guide.

'They are,' the seller agreed. 'That's good. I think you are learning some of their ways. But I give if you take.' It held out a glass of clear liquid.

'I am yours and you are mine. And so is my friend.'

The guide took another glass and gave it to Fosse, earning a stare from the seller, and they drank. It was like the stuff he had been drinking since his own water supply ran out, but stronger, with a sharp edge that sent heat coursing down his throat. Then they returned the glasses and the seller moved back to his position.

'It's a shame this place is falling down,' said Fosse.

'It doesn't matter.'

'Don't you care about it?'

It shrugged. 'Things change. We build, unbuild. Rebuild. Is that a word?'

'So why not rebuild it now?'

'How will we know what it should look like? We must wait for the end. Ha! I shouldn't say it. It's impossible to talk about. Can I ask you a question?'

'Of course.'

'Where do babies come from?'

'Ummm...' said Fosse.

The guide laughed at him. 'Somebody told me that was the most difficult question you can ask a human. Is that true? I heard you squeeze them out of yourselves, and cut them free. They do not decide to come free themselves.'

'Well, no, I mean... they decide when to come out, sometimes.'

'I think that's the worst thing I ever heard about humans.'

'Why?' Fosse asked him, although, when phrased in those terms, he had to accept the guide had a point. 'Isn't that what happens with Qitans?'

'We come all at once. Then nothing for a while. Then more. Then nothing. Then more. Until the end. But in the times we come we are together, a family. We are never alone. You must feel very alone.'

'I do,' Fosse admitted. 'Sometimes.' He realised that, even while having a conversation that should put the act of sex in his mind, he didn't really want to think of it. It was undoubtedly true that it was much easier to live without those thoughts, or with the need to even touch himself, let alone think about touching others. The dampener he'd asked for onboard the ship to Qita was still working, then. He supposed he should be grateful. And yet he felt a sudden pang for the boy he had been, in the barn, staving off loneliness by taking pleasure in his own hands, his own body. Perhaps some emotions were simply very human.

'Feeling alone is odd,' said the guide. It sat back on the bench and stuck out its feet, crossing them at the ankles. 'You belong on Qita in the same way that I belong on Qita, that every traveller belongs here. I think we don't have to move on at speed. Shall we stay here for a while?

I have family in this town. They don't like me much, but they are obligated. Let's see them.'

'All right,' said Fosse. It was very pleasant there, in the shade. 'Why not?'

'But first,' said the guide, 'More brew. More brew!'

SOMETIMES THE GUIDE was an old man, and so was Fosse.

They would sit together on the bench in the square and heckle until they were given brew. They'd talk loudly about all that was wrong with the world, both worlds, any world, and they would be in perfect agreement whether they understood each other or not.

Sometimes the guide was an old woman, and Fosse was a young boy in her presence. She would tell him off for wasting his life, spending all day drinking, even while she was doing exactly the same thing herself. She would snipe at the sellers for being slow, and point out how dirty and dilapidated the square looked. Everything was wrong at those times, and Fosse hated the old woman, and also loved her, when she appeared to him, which was rare.

Sometimes the guide was a young man, looking for trouble, picking up rocks from the rubble and throwing them at the sellers who had refused to serve them. They'd get chased out of the square and then they'd retreat to the house of the guide's long-suffering relatives. These proved to be three Qitans who wove the suits that all Qitans wore from a coarse orange fibre. Their business took up the top floor of the tall house, and they lived on the ground floor, leaving the middle floor for their frequent visitors. None of these relatives spoke any English, and Fosse suspected they all hated him through their silences and avoidances. He felt, when his suspicions got the better of him, like the guide's little brother, dragged unwillingly into mischief, not knowing how to turn things to his advantage.

But sometimes, most rarely, the guide was a little girl. The girl kept a doll in its suit that it brought out and cuddled, just before sleep. The doll resembled an octopus, Fosse thought, although he had never seen it up close. It had many loose limbs that the guide would wrap around her fist as she went to sleep. She would do this only when she had far too much to drink and then had an argument with her family. She seemed to need soothing, then.

'TELL ME A story, please,' the guide said, after one particularly long bout of imbibing brew. It lay on the floor, in the corner they had earmarked as their own, even as the other relatives came and went in their silence, and plucked at the limbs of its doll.

Fosse felt, for a moment, like a father. He sat by the guide and thought of her tenderly, wanting to tell her something that would thrill her without scaring her. It was not difficult to talk, with such emotions inside him.

'Once upon a time,' he said, 'there was a boy who lived in a dark wood and dreamed of running away to a city.' He paused, wet his lips with his tongue, thinking of what he would say, how he would make a beginning and an end and a meaning from it all. 'He met a family who was not like his family, who didn't understand him. The new family took him in and told him that he could be safe there, with them. What he couldn't see was that they were lying to him.' The story was running away with him. It had a life of its own. 'Perhaps they were lying to themselves as well. And then one day he found out about the lies, and he—'

The guide said, 'I don't think I like that story.'

'You don't know what the end is yet!'

'Neither do you. That's not the problem, anyway.' The guide turned over and curled up, the doll clutched close.

'But it's my story,' Fosse said.

'No, it isn't,' said the guide. They did not talk of it again.

*　　*　　*

'No, it isn't,' says a woman's voice, far away, then, 'It is, it is.'

My feet are wet.

I open my eyes and look around the cellar.

More have joined while I've been... sleeping? I don't know what to call the state in which I find Fosse, in his future, or how to even describe the thing we are becoming. Oh, God, look at us. We have heads and arms and legs aplenty. We merge in many places. So many, going back so far, but it scares me beyond measure, and I tell myself I am with Isley, only Isley. We still hold hands, and that alone binds me. I can wiggle my fingers in his grasp. I can also wiggle his fingers in my own grasp. He opens his eyes and wiggles my own fingers in response. We share control. We are one. I feel safer, knowing he is here with me, and he will continue to keep his promise. I am not subsumed, not yet. Could I control the rest of us? Could I nod Freya's head, or wiggle the ears of Bill Sedley, as I've often seen him do after a few brews? Could I wag Bailey's tail, which is the only part of him that sticks out from the blanket of fur that now coats Freya and Won? I'm tempted to try. And, beyond that, the many voices that are disconnected from the physical: can I speak to them? I feel them waiting for me.

A sound from the stairs.

Two women stand there, in wet clothes. They come to me, away from the main bulk of us. One is young and hard, the other older and softer, and they are joined together by their palms. The skin has merged. Their expressions match: they are both wide-eyed, taking us all in.

I know who they are straight away. And I realise they know who I am.

'Is it raining?' I ask them.

'He looks like you,' the older one says.

'Really?' I've not seen the resemblance myself. I've noticed Dom in him more, in the past. But now I have the boy Fosse and the man Fosse both in my head, and the man looks like his own creation. It's harder to see any of us in him.

'He was a good boy,' she says, a little wistfully.

'He killed Cee,' says the younger one, and there is bitterness and fear there.

I can't speak. Fosse is a murderer. I suspected it, and he thought it. How could the man have survived those injuries, so far from help? But it's one thing to think it, and another to know it.

'It wasn't his fault,' says the older one, and their names come from Fosse's memory to mine, hazy, indistinct, with feelings of love, of fear, of guilt, of being too young and too angry to bear.

'It was, it was,' mourns Victoria. 'Cee had a hard time of it, but he never would have hurt the boy. He remembered what it was like to be one. He was trying to make the boy love him.'

'He couldn't make Fosse understand,' Annie says. This is their version of the story we share. I understand that, and I won't try to rip it down. 'My son carries his guilt,' I tell them. I feel it, as keenly as an injury to myself. 'He carries it everywhere.'

Is real forgiveness even possible, for this crime? No. We go on, though.

'We buried Cee in the field,' says Annie, 'and the mud sucked him in, and then it rose, and rose. The farm is gone. The water's been rising higher and higher all over. We came here. We don't know why. Where is he? Where's Fosse now?'

'What day is it?'

'November eighth.'

'He's on a ship,' I tell them. 'Bound for Qita.' *And he's in Langzin Square, a place I know well, drinking brew, never knowing I once sat there too. Once upon a time...* 'Have you seen my brother?'

'We don't know him.'

No, of course. We only saw the man, that day, Dom and I and the others, when we went there and threatened him to leave. The women were not present. But if they haven't seen him, that means Dom didn't return to the farm later, looking for Fosse.

I have another theory.

A theory that makes me want to cry out, with what's left of my humanity.

Dom has realised he cannot save anyone or help anyone. Not this time. And he would never choose to be part of this thing we're becoming. It's not Protectorate-certified, is it? It's not preserving or crystallising our old ways, keeping us separate and safe. The liquid rises and transforms everything it touches, and there is no room for cream teas and pasties and home-grown goodness and standing for something pure and untainted.

So he'll be up high somewhere, standing on his own for those things. Proud and alone; he'd rather be that way, than together, with us all. I have to admire him. I like that theory, even though it means he has abandoned both me and Fosse. The magnificent and indefatigable Dom. The Protectorate lives on in him, and will never be defeated.

What does this mean?

Perhaps it means I've accepted the fact I'm beyond saving.

I hear a soft, high sound of loss. It's coming from me. I'm making it.

The brown, swirling water is rising. From my position it

looks as if it bulges upwards around the place where Bailey meets Won and Freya; Won's knees are nearly covered.

If we at the inn are sinking, then nearly everything else for miles around must be submerged. I picture the village, lost to the liquid. The calmness of it. The spire of the church sticking out, maybe. Where has everyone gone? Are more people coming here? How many of us can we fit inside this cellar, as part of our mass? Why here, of all places?

'Don't worry,' says Isley. 'We'll all fit.'

He knew my thoughts. Or perhaps he was answering a question from the women that I didn't hear, because Annie says, 'Where?'

'Here, you can come here,' says a voice in the far corner. I can't see past the rest of us to see who's speaking, but my guess is it's Geoff Dyer. There's something in the tone that's familiar. 'Or here,' says Ailsa Wells, a little closer to me. I crane my head to catch a glimpse of her shoulder and neck, facing down, away from me, sloping into someone else. When did they arrive? How much have I missed?

'There's a choice?' says Victoria.

'There's always a choice,' Isley says, but just as I can move his fingers, I can tell that there's a lot being left unsaid, or perhaps *untranslated* would be a better term. Things are being lost between languages.

'Sort of a choice,' I say, thinking of the creatures at Toulu. I thought they were part of the natural process of becoming, but my son's experiences have made it clear: to refuse the Qitans is to die. I don't know how death would come, but it's a fact that must inform the choice for any intelligent creature.

'There are no secrets now,' says Won.

She's right. There are no secrets. I see her now and understand her. She's not a her, she's not a him, she's not a traveller, she's not a threat. There are no fixed points in her at all. She says

I was born one of many, all at the same time, same creation, and I searched for meaning and for separation from my siblings. I could not find something that made me special or unique—as if value lies in exceptionality! I found others who felt the same way, and this is where the confusion begins, the business of wanting to be other together. How does that even work? It works by starting groups and sharing ideas. We shared the concept of freedom between us, finding passion in it without ever having to describe it or find real consensus. It was a murky idyll that could hold us all. We fought so hard to maintain it.

Then the gate opened.

Humans arrived in the sky and came to land, and

some Qitans gathered and welcomed them at Shanlingu, because they represented the beginning of the end. But my family did not welcome them, because we did not want the end to come. We gathered outside the gates of the human base and watched them. They were not joined. They were separate, and they accentuated their differences and cherished them: different words, different clothes, different names. We took on their habits and gave ourselves human names, based on aspects of their culture. I was Wonton, like a taste, a food. Something to be enjoyed. My friend chose the name Isley, after a human song he liked. A summer breeze. We ate up their cultures. We learned their languages, the stranger the better.

Some of us even made it to Earth.

But we could not help but bring some of ourselves with us, and that began to bleed into humanity. It seems there are no differences after all. We are the same, we are the same, and we can take the best of everywhere and make it one. That is not where we began. But it is where we will end, and it's not so bad. We get to become the things we love. We get to become you, and you get to become us, and there is always change and everything is the same.

*   *   *

'YOU'VE CHANGED,' SAID the guide. 'You're ready.'

'For what?'

'Come on,' it said. 'Let's go. There is one last place on this journey.'

Walking again, onwards, out of the town without a word of goodbye, Fosse felt soft and achy. The straps of his backpack dug into his shoulders. He had no idea how long he had spent at Langzin. He had a fine beard, that he liked. He wondered if time could be measured in a human way by the inches of growing hair, but he had no clue how to work it out, and it didn't matter anyway.

There were many more Qitans on the track, which was muddy, although it never rained. Perhaps it was caused by the sheer amount of feet pounding on the ground, wearing it down. Fosse remembered how the liquid had been only just under the surface at the mine. It sparked a memory of home: seagulls dancing on the grass of the village green to mimic rainfall, patting their webbed feet so the worms would rise up. How strong and clear their footfalls must have sounded from under the ground, like a summoning drum.

He was getting better at seeing things from a different angle. It was a matter of distance. He could look back at his home and feel all the things he hated to feel. But there was also acceptance, now. He had come to the realisation that he killed Cee. That he alone was responsible. There was no escaping it, no penance he could do. Part of him, the boy of him, would always be in that moment of the worst thing he would ever do, feeling it, screaming to make a better decision.

That couldn't happen, of course. Nothing could change.

But there was movement onwards.

He imagined returning to Tung Base with so many vibrant images in his head for them to use: keys that could unlock a new level of understanding between Qitan and human. In his fantasy of return, his uncle waited for him, standing outside the main gates. They would hug. It wouldn't need words. Although Fosse found he was not as afraid of words as he had once been.

So many Qitans walked in convoy.

There was singing. Their own language. The few that spoke English came to him and delighted in practising their skills. The guide watched these enthusiastic interchanges benevolently, but with close attention. Fosse thought it felt protective of him.

The English speakers asked him questions, and he asked questions back in return. The answers never quite made sense, but then, the questions didn't either.

'What is yellow?' one asked.

'It's the colour of the sun and some flowers,' said Fosse. 'It makes me happy, but I wouldn't wear it myself. Too bright.'

'No, no, no, yellow,' it said. 'Yellow.' As if he hadn't understood the concept.

'What's yellow to you?'

'It sinks in only so much, like a puddle,' it replied. How different its concept of colour was; he could have spent an age trying to get to the heart of it, but the guide intervened with a long explanation about rainbows on Earth, which only seemed to confuse everyone even more. Still, it was entertaining.

Another time, a very short Qitan with flatter facial features and scalier skin said, 'What are those?' while pointing at Fosse's shoes.

'Shoes,' he said, very clearly, as if talking to a young child.

'I thought they were regulation standard military Coalition issued walking apparel,' it said.

It was strange how being more precise with language could move everyone further away from a mutual level of understanding.

MORE QITANS JOINED in streams, tributaries feeding into a large, snaking river across the land. Nobody went hungry or thirsty. The suits produced sticks and liquid for everyone. The ones who could not walk well, or at all, wore stiffer suits that held them upright, and others pushed or pulled them along.

He thought often of what the guide had told him about bloodshed and killing amongst their kind. He couldn't imagine it. But he thought they probably wouldn't believe it was true of him, either. At times he wished he could say: *I'm a killer.* Would it make things better, to have it said? But it would lead to a question he could not answer.

Why did you kill?

Why had he killed? Why had he not run away, or refused to rise to fear and anger? The only response he could have given would have been a shrug, and an admission that it was simply in his nature. Human nature.

Which meant he had to accept it was part of Qitan nature, too.

THEY WALKED OVER a range of hills, and then through long fields of swaying plants. The guide had told him it was travelling to its end, and he had thought that meant death. Now, he wasn't so sure. These were not all old Qitans, he suspected. Some seemed very young to him, like the one that had asked about his shoes. Some others behaved like parents, feeding and helping, corralling.

It took a long time to get up the courage to ask the guide, 'What is at the end?'

It reached out and took his hand as they walked, side by side. Fosse didn't repeat the question. He could tell the guide was thinking hard by the way it squeezed his hand in time with their footsteps.

Eventually it spoke.

'Zay Shines,' it said.

THEY CROSSED A forest, crested a hill, and looked down over the slopes of the dunes that led to a long beach and a vast expanse of sea.

The beach was white, and the surface was cracked, as if the sand had fused in heat. It was covered in Qitans; thousands of them. They had all set up their own tents from their suits, and placed poles in front of themselves: 'To mark their place,' said the guide, 'but not for much longer.'

Fosse's uncle had liked to walk the beaches at home on their camping holidays. He had once described the sight of an influx of holidaymakers, back before the borders to the Protectorate had closed to such damaging pursuits. *Every inch taken up with plastic and rubbish and bodies covered in sun cream,* he had said. *And more in the water, swimming, even when there's no room left to swim.*

Nobody swam here. The sea was empty and calm, waveless. Humps, too smooth to be rocks, punctuated the smooth surface. There were tens, hundreds of them. They were random, scattered.

'What happens now?' Fosse asked.

The guide said, 'We will go down and make our choice.' They started forward; there was no way to stop, in the movement of the column, the crush of bodies. They had to go down, get closer. He realised the top of each round tent bore a swirling pattern.

'I don't know,' he said. 'I don't like it.' He let go of the guide's hand. They had got into the habit of walking along that way, and it felt wrong to be without its reassuring grip. The skin of their palms stuck together, sweaty and moist, then came apart.

'You're scared?'

'Yes.'

'We won't rush. We can sit at the back.'

The guide was true to its word. As they approached the bottom of the dunes, the path widened and they were able to break from formation, moving along the back of the beach until they found a place with very few tents pitched, far from the main crush.

The guide said, 'Here,' and began the task of turning

its suit into a tent. Once the tent was constructed, it pulled out a long pole from the sand itself—it extended vertically, dripping with liquid, hardening into place as it dried—and marked its spot. Then there was nothing to do but sit down and wait; the guide, only in its undergarments, sat cross-legged, and lifted up its arms to the sky for a long time. Then it sighed, dropped its arms, and said, 'We are here.'

'This is the end?'

'Not yet. Almost.'

'Should I go?'

'If you want to.'

'Do you think I should?'

It looked at him steadily. 'No,' it said. 'I don't think I want you to go. You can stay here with me.'

'Nobody else has more than one at their tent.'

'I told you already,' said the guide. 'I'm old and I don't care.' It held out its hand. Fosse sat down. They waited together.

THEY WERE HAVING a long conversation about beetles when Fosse stood up, realising the Qitans had begun to walk into the sea.

The guide had asked him to describe as many different kinds of beetles as he could, and had then puzzled over what they had to do with The Beatles. Apparently, someone on the base had been playing music by The Beatles and the guide had heard it. Beatles beetles, said the guide. It was an absorbing and inconsequential conversation, which Fosse had learned was his favourite kind.

He got up to stretch and saw them in the water.

'Swimming!' he said to the guide, and made the windmill gesture.

'No,' said the guide, and Fosse looked more closely, and saw how the Qitans walked straight out without pause, further, further, until the liquid closed over their heads and they were gone.

They did not resurface.

More followed. The beach was emptying. Thousands were walking into the sea.

'The end,' said the guide.

'I don't understand. Stop them. Stop them.'

'You can't change their choice. What's your choice? Are you coming with us?'

'Don't go,' Fosse said, in terror, in desperation.

'That's my choice. I go in, I join. Then we are we, together, and much later we break apart to make new shapes, new forms. And it begins again.'

'Don't go!'

'I want to.'

'No, it must be something in the water, in the liquid. It makes you think that you want to—it's not you...'

'It's us.'

'No, the liquid is alive, it's your enemy, it forces you to—'

'It is us. We are the liquid. We come from the liquid. And yes, it is alive, because it is part of us.' The guide stood up and put its hands on Fosse's head, over his ears. 'Be calm, be calm,' it said. 'This is not terrible. It's wonderful. You are so young, I forget, I forget how young you are and that you are scared, and I will wait until you are ready. Come, or go. Your choice. Sit. Here.'

They both sat down again.

Fosse's terror began to ebb. He closed his eyes. It was better when he couldn't see the procession into the sea.

The guide sang in its own language, and time passed.

BUT TIME WOULD not stop: not for Fosse, not for anyone. He opened his eyes and saw how few Qitans there were left. The sea had taken nearly all of them.

'What's happening to them now?' Fosse asked.

The guide said, 'Together.'

'Changing into one?'

'Yes.'

'You don't really want to change, do you?'

'Change comes anyway,' it said. 'Doesn't it?'

Fosse couldn't argue with that.

'It's time,' it told him. 'Are you ready?'

'No,' he said, but he realised that wasn't quite true. He had made his decision, and simply didn't want to admit it to himself. 'Yes.'

'Good.' The guide stood, and Fosse did too. They looked out over the sea, at the last Qitans entering, and the once smooth humps that were beginning to swell up into tall, lumpy columns. Fosse didn't want to see them up close. He wished, for one moment, for his axe. Then he pushed that thought away, as unworthy of the human he hoped to become. He said, 'I'm going. Back to Tung Base. I want to show them what I've recorded, so we can understand each other better.'

'Even though there will be none of us left, in the shape that you know?'

It was too much to take in. He stuck to what he could understand. 'You could come with me. Help me to explain it. We'll walk back along the route with all the leaflets. The white path.'

The guide laughed. Its tongue lolled out. 'Not now,' it said. 'But listen. I will leave a place for you, here, beside me. You are part of me, and I am part of you. I will not forget that, even when I'm one and many.'

'You won't forget me?' Fosse asked. He was the man and the boy, both, in that question.

'I won't,' the guide promised, and put its forehead to his. Fosse felt their skin join, fuse, and it was not some awful disease but a gift, a gift he wanted to keep. But the guide pulled away and their skin separated.

'Will you watch me walk in?' it said.

'Of course.'

It walked down the beach, an old soul, bent and slow, carrying a heavy life. It did not even pause when it reached the sea. It shuffled in until the liquid covered its knees, its pouchy stomach, then the loose muscles of its chest. To its chin. Up over its head.

Fosse watched for a good while.

When he felt certain it was done, he packed up the tent into a suit, and stripped off his dirty uniform to put the suit on. It did not really fit, at first, but as he began to walk back along the beach, then over the dunes, he felt it moulding to his body. It started to cling to him, to come to know him, as a friend.

He walked.

The suit made food and liquid for him in endless supply. When he cried, it created a lip under his chin, as if trying to catch and preserve the tears for him. It felt like a closeness to the guide, to wear it. Alone, together. Together, alone.

*   *   *

'THEREFORE WHAT GOD has joined together, let man not separate.'

The words come to me and shake me loose from the future.

Reverend Sumner stands on the stairs, halfway up to keep out of the liquid, stooping so she can see us all.

'Really, Vicar?' says one of us. It's Michael Frescombe. I can't see him. There are many of us now, a bulk of us, and some parts I recognise more easily than others. Doctor Clarke's thinning hair is close by. His fight is over. I feel so sad for him, for what he was. His belief in a complete and protected village, an encapsulation of a dream, is done with.

How much time has passed while I've been away with my son?

There's an arm that looks familiar, but I can't place it. Perhaps one of the local darts team. Michael Frescombe's head must be on Won's other side, building out from her. I can still see Bailey's tail, wagging away. And I think that's Klaus' leg, extending out in front, long and lean. Michael will be next to Klaus, of course.

The bodies without, so many voices within.

'I couldn't help it,' says Reverend Sumner. 'It feels like a union.'

'So you had to bless it?' But Michael doesn't sound angry so much as amused.

She hesitates, then whispers, 'It is not good that the man should be alone.'

'Genesis, right?' Michael says, then, 'There's a space for you here.'

'Thank you,' she says. She comes down the stairs, wading to her place beside him and Klaus, and all of us. She repeats, 'Man should not be alone,' as she joins us.

The fight is leaving me. The fight is nearly ended.

To be alone was not a new experience for Fosse, but this time around it was worse for being his choice. He had chosen to return to his own kind. His own kind: a strange phrase. It didn't quite fit him anymore.

He wondered often if he'd made the right decision, particularly when he looked around himself and did not quite recognise the landscape. Was he walking in the right direction? He wanted to find his path organically, much as the guide did. But then it occurred to him that it had only *seemed* easy from the outside, not knowing how it was achieved. He simply hadn't understood that aspect of the guide's life, along with so much else of it.

With that revelation, he realised he did not want to be human any more. The struggle inherent in it—blinded to so much, filled with the noise of his own existence that deafened him to all else—disgusted him. He nearly turned around many times, but for some reason he kept moving forward. In places, the path looked familiar, but altered: a town emptied, or a field of orange flowers turned pink. Eventually he came to a place that he was certain he had been before. The abandoned Coalition mining facility surrounded by fencing. He approached it slowly. The front gates were still locked, but the tunnel the guide had dug had been filled in, or had perhaps sealed itself over. Beyond the fence were the military buildings, and the vast barrel on the tall tripod.

The barrel stored the liquid. The brew, the sea.

So that was the business of the Coalition: drilling, and taking the liquid for use on Earth. To do what? The guide had said that Qitans *were* the liquid, and the liquid was brew. There was a life cycle happening here. Fosse had no idea if the Coalition had any inkling of that connection. He didn't see how they could. But they knew how to make a profit, and brew did that. His uncle had warned him against trying it, never touching the stuff himself. His mother had drunk it freely, every night at the Skyward Inn, with many of the locals—literally drinking the bodies of Qitans. He wondered what that might do to her. To all the people back on Earth.

He began to understand. The hands, the disease, the

joining and separating.

The final stretch of the journey back to base, along the highway, did not take long. He walked fast. He had to return to explain what was happening before he lost himself completely.

THIS JOURNEY IS not quite over yet, not for me, not for my son. We go on. Together, apart.

'Jem?'

I know that voice. Benny Sykes. I open my eyes and search the darkness for him. He's high up on the stairs, crouching—not one of us, yet. There's no room for him to descend further. We take up all the space, at least on Won's side. Isley has protected me and preserved me. He's true to his word, and we are still only joined by our hands, although I could sink into him without a moment's thought, and love being part of him and his generations forever. Hardly anything in me resists any longer. My horror at this creation is old, weary. It wants to be done with.

'Hello, Benny,' I say.

'Jem, you look, you look—like you.'

'You old charmer,' I tell him. An old manner comes back to me easily; it's the business of being a barmaid. 'You here for a brew?'

'I'm not.'

'Did you know brew is made of Qitans? From Qitans?' I tell him. I want him to understand what happened. 'They're the same stuff, or something. I suppose it's all mingled in with our own water, now.' Yes, the water, now up to my waist. Soon it will cover us completely. 'If I'd known that, I might have drunk a few less.'

'Me too,' he says.

'You joining?' I ask him.

'I don't know. I want to, I think. Something made me come up here, to join.'

'It's not as scary as it looks,' I tell him. Bodies, limbs, heads, all joined, rearranged. Monstrous. I remember Reverend Sumner's marriage ceremony—how long ago was that? I'm losing all track of time. She's part of us now; she's happy and drowsing, and she feels love. For us, from us.

'Jem,' Benny says again, and I know that tone. I have been hiding from it in my barmaid ways, but I knew it as soon as he said my name the first time.

'Tell me.'

'Dom's dead.'

Fosse knew it the moment he reached the end of the highway and found the gates of Tung Base unguarded, open. In his imagination that had been the spot where his uncle had been waiting for him. There was nothing. Only a feeling, deep down inside from a dark place, that a small voice had said terrible words softly, kindly, and made it real to him. The base was silent, and his uncle was dead.

He sat down on the road and curled up tight, hugging his knees. The suit puffed up around him into a protective ball. He pulled his arms and legs inside it, and felt a small, soft object against his chest: the guide's doll.

He clutched it tight, closed his eyes and slept.

'JEM, OPEN YOUR eyes,' says Benny.

I pull back from my son. Barely a moment could have passed. But how long this time has seemed, since finding out Dom is gone. An age has gone by, and I am very much older.

'We found Dom out by the Valley Farm. The illegals out there were making traps. Pits, with sharpened stakes at the bottom. It looks like Dom fell into one and a stake went through his thigh. He couldn't get out again.'

I picture him there, and something in me is screaming. He was all I had left to keep me in this world. 'You found him.'

'Why would he have gone out there alone?'

'Looking for Fosse,' I tell him. That was his first and last thought, every day. To protect his nephew. His family. 'Fosse is alone. *Was* alone. What day is it?'

'It's the end of November. Dom must have been out there on his own for... a while. We couldn't get him out of the pit, Jem. The water's been rising fast.'

I hold on to Fosse, to the time to come. In the future, Fosse is alive and well. Dom would have wanted that knowledge, at the end. I wish I could give it to him.

'The disease is everywhere,' says Benny. 'There's word that they're going to bomb the entire Protectorate. Bomb it clean.'

'That won't work,' says Isley, suddenly. He sounds very sure.

Another voice says, 'It doesn't matter.' It sounds like a child. We are so big, and I don't know the half of us. I am consumed by the future, and have no time for this present. Let it swallow me whole.

'He was a good brother,' I tell Benny, tell all of us. I want him to be remembered that way. I feel many things from the bulk of us. Sympathy, pain, sorrow. Guilt, too, from Annie and Victoria, and their part in this loss. They, of course, know exactly what loss is like.

But something stops me from sinking myself entirely into us.

I could choose to let all of my feelings and their feelings

intermingle. I could let it all seep into the bulk of us and be absorbed, and lessened. It is miniscule compared to the suffering we have seen over time and space. Isley squeezes my hand. He wants to take me into himself and take the pain away. This is the moment when I could let that happen.

This is my choice.

Before I do, I have to see it all. I have to know what comes next, for my son.

FOSSE WALKED THROUGH empty corridors to the packing bay. The shelves were stacked and the loaders still showing charge. The base generators were working.

Coach might still be active.

Long out of practice, he tried to access the presence in his head. Nothing happened. No work overlay, no schedule. Of course—it had been turned to silent mode for his travels. It would probably take someone of a much higher rank to unblock it.

Or there was no longer any Coach left at all.

The fear that everyone had returned to Earth and forgotten him, leaving him trapped, hit him hard. He called out, 'Hello?' The sound reverberated around the bay, then died away. There had to be someone, somewhere; he stuck to the familiar walkways of the refectory, the gym, calling out, periodically trying to find any sort of interface or augmentation. But the gym was a drab, utilitarian space. He tried to picture it as a jungle, as a circus. The equipment looked old and greasy, and smelled of stale sweat.

His room held not the slightest evidence of humanity. His few possessions were missing, but it seemed nobody else had replaced him. The bedding had been stripped and the mattress smelled damp.

Fosse opened his desk drawer. It was there, small and sharp: the splinter from the handle of his axe. He took it in his hand, and held it tight as he turned away.

Eventually he ended up at Human Relations. He shouldn't have gone in unaccompanied—that was protocol. It made no difference any more. The doors were all unlocked, and he walked down the corridors searching for the small meeting room where he had first accepted his mission to explore Qita. It was impossible to tell, so in the end he simply chose one that looked right, and entered.

The lights came on and the wall flickered into life, showing an aerial view of a coastal megacity. He remembered it. This could be the actual room. Why did that feel like it might make a difference? Everything human was still missing.

He remembered how the man—Li Zhou—had

summoned forth information by drawing on the desktop with his finger. He sat in Li Zhou's seat, and ran his hands over the surface, hoping to activate something. A double tap of the finger, then drawing a symbol, trying to recall it. He ended up drawing a swirl. It was the only shape in his head.

Nothing happened.

Whatever secrets could be unlocked that way were not open to him.

Or perhaps it was not just Tung Base that was empty. Once Fosse had thought about it, he couldn't escape it. Whatever had happened to the base might not be an isolated incident. It could have happened on Earth. Not just to the Coalition, but to everyone. To the Protectorate...

'No, no, no,' he told himself. He sounded like the guide, and that was enough to get him out of the chair and moving. He retraced his steps and then went outside to the spaceport, to find only a few Coalition ships lined up there. Some people had managed to make the choice to leave.

Fosse kept the splinter of the axe in one hand, and took out the guide's doll to hold in the other. He went back inside and made his way down to the maintenance facilities in the basement.

* * *

YES, THERE WERE people there, alive and joined in liquid, one main body of merged heads and torsos and mouths and eyes, and long snaking arms and legs reaching out, hands clasping and releasing, stretched up in joy.

Voices spoke in many languages: Chinese, Russian, Urdu, Swahili, Spanish, and the singing of Qitans. He finally understood that Qitan song sounded like a harmony because it was exactly that—made up of so many other languages, each one added and incorporated.

'English,' said Fosse.

'We become,' said a voice.

'We're together,' said another, from another part.

'Li Zhou?' Fosse asked.

'I'm here.'

He could not see a head for Li Zhou, but the voice sounded familiar.

'It's the end,' said Fosse. 'Isn't it?'

'We join and combine our cells. Then we'll break apart and spread out again. Next time we'll be part human, too.'

'Is it the same as Zay Shines? I went there. I saw it. I have it all in my head.'

'That's right, I sent you to find out, didn't I? We knew something was happening. We have no need of that information now.'

'So it wasn't to increase understanding at all, then? My mission. I was a spy.'

Many voices laughed. 'It doesn't matter now,' a woman said.

'Not even on Earth?'

'No. Not even there.'

Fosse felt his legs tremble. He was very tired. 'Is this all over Earth as well, then?'

'It is.'

So it was all gone. The many kinds of people, of life, the Coalition, the Protectorate, the languages, the religions, the differences. All combined to one type of being: this mass of flesh.

'It's murder,' he said.

'Many feel that way, and they haven't been taken into us. It's a choice. Even though they will try to kill us now, it's still their choice.'

'Nothing will be lost,' said the guide, from the depths of the body, and the sound of that familiar voice made Fosse so happy, so sad. 'All the words and all the thoughts are here, but now there is no space between them. It's good. It's perfect.'

'I don't want it to be perfect.' He liked the gaps more than the meanings.

'You don't have to join,' the guide said. 'Just like at Zay Shines. It is still your choice.'

'Is that true?' he cried. He held out both the doll and the splinter of the axe, showed them to the mass. 'Which is right?'

'It's complicated,' said his mother's voice. 'I know, it's really complicated. But I think it's better than being alone, or being dead.'

'All the bodies join together.'

'The minds too. Across space and time.'

'How does that work?'

'Take my hand,' said his mother, 'and I'll tell you.'

'I don't know. I don't know.'

'Take my hand,' she said again, and he saw her hand, a very human hand, emerge from the mass and extend out towards him. The sight of it made him a boy again. He could not be alone, and he could not be a killer. Not again.

He dropped the doll and the splinter and took her hand.

'Isley,' I say, in the darkness.

'I'm here.'

It's warm. I'm floating in liquid up to my chin. It's buoyant; I don't need to work at staying comfortably upright. My eyes adjust. My face is only a few inches below the cellar's ceiling. There are hundreds of physical beings here with me, pressing into the walls, and millions in my mind, but Isley is true to his word and has curled himself around me to keep me separate from the main mass. His eyes and mouth are close to my face, and they look the same to me. I don't know how much else of him is left.

'Alone at last,' he says. 'Fancy a brew?'

There's a long creaking from the walls, and sighing from us. He's still holding my hand.

'No, thanks,' I say. 'I have a suspicion about how you make that stuff.'

'Hmm. I didn't think you'd want to know.'

'Please tell me I haven't been drinking your pee.'

'Well, when demand outstripped supply I started bringing in Won's pee as well.'

'Jesus!'

'I diluted it with water,' he says. 'Unless it was just for us two.'

'It passed through your body. It's part of you.'

'So what? Aren't humans half water?'

'I think it's more than that,' I admit.

'I've been thinking a lot about when humans first came to Qita,' he says. 'I was at Shanlingu, you know. Holding up a welcome sign. Messages of welcome were given out from both sides, but neither side really meant it in the way the other thought. Earth wasn't actually giving Qita a choice at all. It's all so silly, really.'

'It could so easily have been war.'

'It *is* war! The Coalition is fighting us right now. Well, bits of the Coalition. The ones who didn't want to join. They won't be content to leave us alone.'

'You didn't want to join,' I remind him.

'We're all entitled to change our minds. It doesn't matter, anyway.'

'You've said that before. You all say that.'

'It's true, Jem. It's so silly to think otherwise. It's very human, I think.' He says the word *human* with such casual fondness. 'And it isn't just a case of you and me anymore. If it was, one could say—*you tried to conquer us* and the other could say—*you knew it would change us*. It doesn't lead anywhere.'

I think of Fosse's memories to come. The tripod, and the barrel. 'So the Coalition didn't know what the liquid was when they started bringing it to Earth?'

He says, very quietly, 'It doesn't matter.'

'It does to me!'

'There's no conspiracy theory. They aren't the enemy of you, or the Protectorate. There is no enemy. Just beings, trying to live.'

'That's the stupidest thing you've ever said to me, and I'm counting the time you asked me if the expression *bottoms up* came from a period when everyone had to stand on their heads to drink.'

'You are never going to let that go, are you?' he says.

'That, and the pee drinking.'

'I didn't think the end would come, here, to Skyward. It was just me, and you. So far from home. And when you drank brew you told such wonderful stories, so well, so strongly. Not real stories, but I could see how you saw me, my planet. As perfection. I told myself just the two of us could never trigger the end. But then Won couldn't leave, and I realised that brew was everywhere, in the water, making its changes. Perhaps it was putting it all together that made it start. I don't know. I was stupid, too. See? It's not just a human trait. I never wanted this to happen, but it did, it has, and now I see it's not really an end but—'

'I don't understand,' I tell him.

'Come inside me. Let me come into you, and you will.'

I want to.

My choice.

If it were just Isley, I would choose to be with him.

But his words remind me of Fosse, and the future.

'Dom. His body was in the liquid too, before he died. Benny said so.' Yes, I can access Benny's memories through the mass of us, now. I walk through the woods, taking my time, wary, and I come to a square cut pit, it must have taken a lot of work, and inside it, I find him, small and broken. Liquid in him, over him. I don't want to look too closely. His eyes are open. He's not seeing.

His fingers are ruined. He left deep gouges in the earth, and his leg is destroyed. Dom.

'He didn't join,' says Isley, with such sadness. 'He didn't want to. Everyone has a choice.'

'Sort of.' Because choosing not to join is choosing loneliness, and that is very hard to do. We humans fight each other so hard, and most of all we fight being alone wherever we find it. I wonder if Dom understood what the liquid offered him: a solution to it all. A way of living forever in which we combine and separate, over and over. Rearrangement, and togetherness.

Somehow, he found the will to turn it down. I wonder what he hung on to. Possibly it was the idea of the Protectorate: his home. His only love.

'I love you,' whispers Isley. 'I grieve with you. But this is not your home, nor Dom's home. None of us has a home. Not Earth. Not Qita. A new gate will open soon, and we'll go there. Nobody belongs to only one place.'

'A new gate?'

'The gates open and close. When the Kissing Gate appeared and linked our planets, we were ready for you. Gates come and go, Jem. We travel, and we intermingle. All of us are one. Not just Qitans and humans. Every creature, everywhere.'

'Qita wasn't your home planet?'

'No! Of course not. We journey. We travel.'

I can't picture it. It goes against everything I thought I knew of the Qitans. They are so peaceful, and yet they are the conquerors of worlds. 'Show me,' I say. 'Show me where you started, and where this ends.'

'Try not to think of it as—'

'Please.'

I close my eyes and see

ZAY SHINES.

Or any place, on any world, made anew, turned into the soft, quiet land with the light breeze and the still liquid of life. The new beings come free from the diminishing columns. They wade to shore, soft and stumbling. But their skins harden. They have arms and legs and heads. They are a combination of all that lived before on that world, and chose to be transformed, to live again.

The time of the beings that did not choose to join has passed. The liquid made them infertile. Their old methods of reproduction ceased to work, and by the time recombination had been completed, they had become part of the soil.

There are thousands of new beings spreading out, across the land, and time. We speed ahead, and the beings are making settlements and settling down with their siblings. Maybe this time they will have found contentment in combination, which is all they seek. A world somewhere must hold the secret of how to make togetherness without pain possible.

But it was not this world.

They are at war within themselves already. They are so many creatures rolled into one and it is hard to be so many things, and that war spreads. They start to kill each other for little or no reason. This is no paradise. The corpses melt to liquid and trickle to the sea, and it doesn't matter. They'll be born again, next time around. The dead wait for new beings to come from the sky, to take them back to their own planet. Then the columns will call from the liquid, and all war will stop. It will be time to combine again.

You will come into me, and we will combine again. Alone and together, forever.

Was that Earth's future?

The voices in my head tell me gently that I've seen the future of all worlds, eventually, but I can't hope to understand the joy of it until I join. I push them all away and turn only to Isley. He's still with me. We can still be the two of us, and I can still use the words of my own language.

I ask him, 'Who makes the gates appear and disappear?'

'I can't explain it, Jem.' I can hear the sheer effort in his voice to speak to me this way. 'Join, and have your answers.'

'But if I join, I won't care about the answers, will I?'

Isley sighs. All of us sigh, and the walls of the cellar groan, long and low.

'Tell me now!'

'This... there's no way to... look. You know those nights when we'd be full, and there would have been a darts match, and everyone had drunk all the brew they wanted? They'd start singing, but it would be out of tune, and there'd be different words in different places, and nobody could agree on what they were meant to be? Like "Harmless Molly." Like that. But complete. All the words, all the tunes, all out of time, all at once. But there's no doubt it's the same song. The makers of the gates are the song.'

I stop myself from saying the obvious. Isley says, 'I know. You don't understand.'

'I never have.'

But I will. In Fosse's future, I do understand, already, and I will urge him to join because of that. I will hold out my hand, our hand, and he will take it. Because I know there can be no future for him any other way.

That's what breaks me. The idea that I'm already destined to say such a thing to him.

I can't accept that.

The bulk of us feels my decision, and Isley says, 'We came to Skyward to be together. That's the truth. That's what this is.'

'Together alone,' I tell him.

'Together alone is better than alone alone.'

'That doesn't make any sense.'

'Don't,' he whispers, but I'm done. The price of understanding is to no longer care. I can't do that. I want to care about my brother's death. I want to care about what I'll say to my son, and how important it is that he makes his own decisions, good or bad, whatever they may be. I thought good and bad didn't matter, but it turns out it does to me. To whatever I am, whatever I remain.

'Let me go.'

'I don't want to.'

'That's not your choice.'

The bulk of us begs. We call out my name: a name I'll lose if I stay. But we are true to ourselves. We do not force. We let go.

'We had the part,' says a voice. I know it from the past. She came to the Skyward, showed me a map. Then we met at Wrecker's Cave, and she stole our only hope of avoiding this. 'We had the part you needed, all along.'

'It's okay,' I tell her, but she shows me an image. She's

strident about it. The part, and the suit, and how they fit together.

Could it be a chance at a different future?

I thank her. I thank all of us. Isley lets go of my hand. Our skin separates slowly. With reluctance. With pain. I have to return to pain.

My buoyancy leaves me. I sink deep into the muddy liquid. It's too thick to swim through. I take a breath in panic and my mouth is filled, my nostrils and eyes clogged. I'll die. I'm dying.

Everything moves sideways, and I'm carried out, and up, and thrown clear of the liquid, into too-cold bright air.

I cough, and scrape at my eyes and nose until I can breathe again. The light is so painful that it takes a long time until I can bear to look around me. I'm on the grass outside what remains of the inn. Rising from its wreckage is a column of life. Not just human life: I can see many different animals sunk into the swaying mass: foxes, badgers, squirrels. Insects, too. Studded, gleaming black beetles and red flashes of ladybirds, writhing worms and thrashing fish and the dry diamond patterns of adders. Horses and cows and sheep. Is that Bailey's tail? No, that's back in the cellar. There are many dogs and cats, and birds, too. Feathers and whiskers. It's not even half human. But there are complete human heads, too, dotted here and there, smiling at me. Some faces I know, some I don't. I can't see Isley. I hope he's feeling joy right now. I think maybe he threw me clear when the walls collapsed. I think he saved my life.

I WADE THROUGH the liquid for miles. It covers everything, and the trees rise from its still depths as the only recognisable features. Their branches wave in an odd rhythm; the liquid will be transforming them, too. Purple mountains, white ground, orange swaying plants in an endless breeze. But the ground feels solid under my feet. This is the highest land for miles, along the cliff tops. I have no idea how long it will stay so, but I manage to reach my destination, eventually.

I enter the cave and feel along the rough wall until I find the rock as it was described to me. I roll it back and find the stash in the hole underneath: bottles of brew, strange pieces of machinery, and Won's suit. I unfold the suit and fit the right piece into place. Then I put the suit on, and leave the cave to stand on the cliff edge.

I have no idea how to operate it, but it seems to know what I want. It begins to rise. As it lifts me up, it forms a clear seal over my face. Higher, higher. It angles my body so I can see down over what remains of my home. For it is my home, no matter what Isley or the mass said. It will always be my home.

There are the remains of Skyward, and there's the column erupting from it, getting taller. It's not the only one. I see others, all over the land and coming out of the sea. There's a huge one at the Swansea spaceport.

Up.

I see planes, in the distance. Coalition bombers, maybe.

Please, I beg the suit, *take me to Qita. Take me to find my son.* I've left behind the blue of Earth and now I'm without light, without air, without anyone or anything. I have to hope that I'm heading for the Kissing Gate, and it's still in place. I finally understand what it means to be alone and free of choice. I'm as powerless as a lone voice against a mighty, rousing chorus, and the song, the song will go on.

Harmless Molly

Hark! Hark! the wars call me away
My pretty love I can not stay!
Hark! Hark! the wars call me away
My pretty love I can not stay!
For I must go to fight proud Spain
Although I leave you, although I leave you,
Although I leave you love, do not complain.
Take me on board my love! said she,
Contented I shall be with thee
No storms no perils will I fear
So bold I venture, in battle with my dear.
Harmless Molly! Gentle fair!
From such a risk I pray forbear
Weak woman soon will frighted be.
In honour love I will return to thee.
When wars are over, and all is peace
Our loves & joys will have increase.
Then will I wing me to my turtle dove
In sweet pleasure, without all measure
Will tell sweet prattling tales of love.

Sung by Samuel Fone, Mary Tavy,
23 December 1892